LEFT WITH THE DEAD
A Gathering Dead Novella
By Stephen Knight

NEW YORK CITY

The dead were everywhere.

Gartrell sprinted through the darkened husk of New York City, the flare in his left hand sputtering and spitting as it slowly ran itself down. He felt its heat on his hand even through the heavy glove he wore. Ignoring the sensation, he ran through the night as fast as he could, weaving around abandoned cars and trucks. He avoided the sidewalk and kept to the street itself. The deserted vehicles served as a type of obstacle course, slowing down the tide of corpses that pursued him.

Just the same, it was only a matter of time until they caught him.

The flare sputtered its last, turning into just a glorified sparkler now. Gartrell flung it away. He juked to his right and slid on his ass across the hood of a taxi cab, firming his grip on the Atchisson AA-12 automatic shotgun that hung from his body by its patrol strap. He didn't know how many rounds he had left, but it couldn't be very many. Five? Six? Behind him, past the wall of stenches that pushed through the street after him, he heard the chatter of automatic gunfire. It was the Coast Guard ship's .50 caliber machinegun, holding back the zeds in order for McDaniels and the others to get to safety. He wished them luck. They would need it.

And so did he.

As he ran past an abandoned UPS truck, a stench reached for him, its fingers curled into claws, its jaws spread wide to reveal a dry maw. But like most stenches it was slow, its movements sluggish and not particularly coordinated. Gartrell saved his ammunition and punched the ghoul in the face instead, knocking it onto its ass as he dashed past. He glanced over his shoulder and saw the rest of the zeds no longer pursued him; instead, they clustered around the smoking remains of the flare he had thrown away.

He slowed just a moment and watched the growing crowd through his night vision goggles. Sure enough, they gathered around the flare, shoving against each other, casting about in the darkness. It took Gartrell a moment to figure out what the story was. The zeds were so stupid they had focused their attention on the flare as he had run through the night, and now their unblinking eyes were glare-blind. They equated the flare with food—him—and they had no idea why he wasn't where the flare lay.

Boy, these things really are *stupid.*

And then, as if to prove he wasn't exactly a mental heavyweight himself, a zombie jumped onto Gartrell from behind. It bit down on his helmet, its teeth skidding across the fabric-covered Kevlar. Gartrell spun and lashed out with his left elbow, and the hard pad he wore there caught the zed right in the face with enough force to break its nose. While the ghoul felt no pain—Gartrell knew the stenches responded to nothing but their incessant hunger—the impact was enough to loosen its grip. Gartrell continued his spin while seizing one of the ghoul's wrists with his left hand and pulled it free. The zombie fell into the street behind him, and Gartrell fired one round from his AA-12 into its face. The zed's skull exploded like an overripe watermelon meeting its fate at a Gallagher show.

The shot captured the attention of the pack of zeds huddled around the flare, and with one collective moan, they surged toward him.

Crap.

Gartrell took off at a run again, heading down East 79th Street as fast as he could, weaving around the derelict cars and other debris that choked the street. The skies still flickered overhead as the artillery bombardment to the north continued unabated. The rangy first sergeant looked in that direction, and wondered if he should make for the Army forces there, or try and double back to the boat.

The boat, he told himself.

He ran to the next intersection, moving as quickly as he could. More stenches flooded into the area, and Gartrell finally had to leave the relative cover of the street for the sidewalk. Concealed now only by darkness, he charged up East 79th Street to the intersection with York. He turned right and scurried up York Avenue. He knew the Coast Guard cutter *Escanaba* would likely sail north until it cleared Roosevelt Island, then turn to the right and head back for the Atlantic Ocean. If he could get to East 86th or East 87th streets, he might be able to hail it before it reversed its course.

He ran and ran, his lungs burning, his legs and feet aching. He avoided contact with the stenches wherever he could, and refrained from firing on them unless he was danger close and there was no other way. Smoke tinted the air as well; there were some fires burning somewhere nearby, but he couldn't see them. Clinging to the shadows, he darted from block to block, and employed stealth and night vision as his primary weapons.

But all the streets east of York Avenue were chock full of the dead. They'd been attracted by the cutter's weapons fire, and they now massed along the banks of the East River. It would be practically impossible to return to the riverfront undetected. Getting to the *Escanaba* was pretty much out the window.

Gartrell swore under his breath and conducted a quick perimeter check. A wave of zeds shambled up the street and sidewalk behind him, moving in his direction. They probably couldn't see him, he decided, but they knew he was nearby. And in the dim recesses of whatever passed for their tiny little minds, they knew that time and numbers were on their side. More stenches swarmed down York Avenue from the north. Their numbers were much smaller than those to the south, but Gartrell still didn't like the odds. They rolled down the wide avenue like a filthy tide.

Gartrell tried the doors of a shop, and then the door of an apartment building, but both were locked. He had gone as far as he could. He couldn't fight his way through to the north, south, or east—he didn't have enough ammunition. He just as quickly discarded the notion of killing himself—things weren't that dire yet, but he put a coda on that thought since it might eventually become an option he would have to consider. Only one thing was clear to him right now: He did not want to be eaten by the gathering dead, and that meant he had to get the hell out of Dodge, pronto.

He turned up 86th Street and headed toward Second Avenue. As he crossed the intersection of York Avenue, a zombie appeared right in front of him. It turned toward him and its eyes widened when it saw him in the darkness. There was no opportunity to do anything else but shoot it. Gartrell blew its head off with one shot, then jumped over the carcass and ran up 86th Street. The AA-12's loud discharge captured the interest of every stench in the area, and before he knew it, the intersection behind him was filling with moaning, walking corpses. And ahead, more stenches appeared, hurrying down the street from Second Avenue. Gartrell was caught between two waves of oncoming zombies.

There was only one thing left to do. Hide.

Gartrell dropped to the ground and slid beneath a car parked at the curb. He flipped up his night vision goggles and unstrapped his AA-12 so he could fit beneath the car; with his body armor and the rest of his gear, it made for a very, very tight fit. He reached down with his right hand and drew his Heckler & Koch Mk 23 SOCOM pistol. It took some effort, as he could barely move. Even with the pistol in hand, if the zeds discovered him he had no doubt how he would fare.

Sure gives a new meaning to the term close-quarters combat.

He then remembered that if McDaniels and the civilians made it to the Coast Guard cutter, it would make a lot of sense to contact the major and let him know Gartrell was still alive. He cursed himself for nothing thinking of it sooner, and he keyed his microphone button twice. *Click. Click.*

"Gartrell! Terminator Five, is that you? Over." As hyper-alert as he was, McDaniels' voice sounded louder than usual in Gartrell's ears.

Gartrell keyed his microphone button. *Click. Click.* Two clicks for yes, one click for no—that was how they'd been trained to communicate when voice contact wasn't possible. And with a thousand zombies advancing on the area where Gartrell lay, having a nice easy chat with the major wasn't going to happen.

"Five, this is Six. Can you speak? Over."

Click.

"Five, this is Six. Are you somewhere on 79th Street? Over."

Click.

"Five, are you injured? Have you been bitten? Over."

Click.

"Five, stand by." The radio fell silent, and above the distant pounding artillery, Gartrell listened to the moans of the dead. He heard their footfalls as they shuffled along the street and sidewalk, and from the corner of his eyes he caught vague glimpses of them as they shambled past the car. So far, so good.

Something grated nearby, metal on metal. Gartrell turned his head toward the sound. One of the ghouls had kicked his AA-12. The weapon lay on the street only a few feet away, but the zombies ignored it. Of course, how could they know one of the keys to his continued survival lay at their feet?

"Five, this is Six." McDaniels didn't sound happy. "The Coast Guard won't allow us to come ashore and rescue you. You have to find a place and hole up, over."

Gartrell shook his head. *Are you fucking kidding me?*

Click. Click.

"I'll be back, Gartrell. As soon as I can get some fellow legionnaires or even lightfighters, we'll be back for you. Over."

Click. It was stupid for anyone to come back to New York City just for him. If Gartrell couldn't find his way out, then there was no way anything less than an entire Army Corps was going to be able to rescue him.

"Five, this is Six. We'll be back for you. I'll bring you back to your wife and kids. I swear it."

Apparently, McDaniels didn't see things the same way. Gartrell hit his microphone button once. *Click.*

"Gartrell...we'll be back, Gartrell. You know the code, we never leave our own behind."

Well, you're going to have to this time, major. Gartrell knew McDaniels would continue preaching the party line and espouse Gartrell not to give up hope. Then and again, McDaniels was apparently safe and sound on the Coast Guard cutter, so he could spout those kinds of platitudes and not really know just how ridiculous they sounded to someone on the receiving end. To avoid that, Gartrell switched off his radio.

He flipped down his night vision goggles and slowly checked the territory to either side of the vehicle. Dozens of legs stalked back and forth as the zeds cast about in the darkness, looking for him. Gartrell was completely surrounded, and as soon as the sun came up...

He looked at the Mk 23 pistol in his right hand, and wondered when he would finally have to use it—on himself.

Three loud, long horn blasts cut through the air. The stenches all turned as one to the east and faced the East River. Gartrell wondered what they saw, but his feet were pointed toward the river, and there just wasn't enough room under the car to turn around. But over the rumble of the distant artillery, he heard something else—the rhythmic throb of big diesel engines. The horn blasted again, and the zombies shuffled toward the river.

Gartrell knew it was the *Escanaba* getting underway. Had the horn blasts been intentional on the part of the Coast Guard, or McDaniels? An attempt to draw as many stenches to the shoreline as possible, and give Gartrell a chance? Or was it just Coast Guard procedure?

Whichever, it didn't matter to Gartrell. The horn blasts kept sounding, and the zeds practically fell all over themselves trying to get back to the river. Soon, Gartrell saw no pacing feet on either side of the car. He was, for the moment, alone.

He crawled out from under the vehicle and picked up his AA-12. Keeping to a crouch, he took a moment to make a long scan of the immediate vicinity. He was half a block from Second Avenue, and perhaps four blocks from East River Drive. Looking in that direction, he saw the *Escanaba* was indeed underway; she'd turned around and was heading back to the sea. All along East 86th Street, apartment buildings and small shops stood silent watch over the dark street. It would be dawn soon, and Gartrell knew he had better find some shelter or risk becoming something's breakfast.

Or, more likely, forced to eat his gun and put a bullet in his own brain.

A Starbucks was across the street. He hurried across the traffic-clogged artery, keeping to a crouch, avoiding contact with the zombies wherever possible. Indeed, they were quite fixated on the *Escanaba*'s bleating horn, and that was curious. It seemed anything that might lead them to a food source was worthy of 100% attention.

The door to the Starbucks was, miraculously, unlocked. Gartrell stepped inside slowly, panning his AA-12 from side to side as he walked down the flight of three steps to the main floor. The coffee urns sat silent and cold behind the counter. Pastries were still inside the refrigerated display case, though it had stopped running quite some time ago. Gartrell eyed what he thought were cinnamon coffee cakes with some intent, regretful now that he had abandoned his rucksack and the several Meals Ready to Eat it contained. Not that MREs were even remotely palatable, but a man on the run from the zombie horde needed something to keep him going. The offerings from Starbucks would make a suitable substitute, even if a trifle stale.

And Lord knows the coffee cake's gonna taste better than Meals Rarely Edible…

He turned away from the display case and took a long look around the shop. The NVGs revealed everything in stark, green-and-white detail. To his right, a short hallway that led to a single restroom. Beside that, another door—probably to the utility area. Next to the door he had entered through, an elevator for disabled patrons—not that anyone would be using it in the near future. To his left lay the dining area. Moving slowly, Gartrell stepped around the counter and looked down its length, toward the barista's area. He raised his AA-12 immediately when he saw a figure crouched on the floor there.

It was a woman. A *live* woman, not a zed. He doubted she could see him clearly, but she must have heard him enter the store; while Gartrell had moved as stealthily as possible, the coffee shop was as silent as a tomb, and even the small noises of his movements stood out. She was dressed in clean, faded jeans, Nike running shoes, and a long-sleeved black T-shirt. Her hair was on the short side, short enough for Gartrell's NVGs to pick up the glitter of the diamond studs in her ears. Her eyes scanned from right to left as she tried to separate his outline from the dark background of the wall behind him. Gartrell cataloged all of these details automatically, but filed them away as tactically irrelevant under the current circumstances. Only one aspect of the sudden encounter commanded his complete attention.

That was the fact she had a gun pointed right at him.

"Lady…do *not* fire that gun. You'll bring every zombie in the neighborhood right to us."

She started at the sound of his voice but didn't scream, didn't make a sound other than a sudden gasp. She clasped the gun in both hands. Gartrell didn't move, kept as still as a statue. When he spoke to her again, he kept low, just above a whisper.

"Relax. I'm a soldier. I'm not going to hurt you. But you have to be quiet, and be calm. There are hundreds of those things right outside."

"I can't really see you," she said after a moment. Her voice quaked, and Gartrell wondered if that was a product of everything that was going on, or if the sudden, chance encounter with another human being had hit her hard.

"I'm right in front of you," he assured her. "I can see you, I have night vision goggles. My name's David Gartrell, and I'm a Special Forces soldier with the U.S. Army. I'm going to come closer to you…all right?"

"Why?"

Gartrell thought that was an odd question, but he answered it anyway. "So I can talk to you and prove to you that I'm human, and that I don't mean you any harm. Or I can just go back to my business and ignore you, if that's what you want." He turned and glanced out the windows. The distant artillery barrage continued, and through the NVGs it looked as if a lightning storm was lighting up the night. In the far distance, he heard the blare of the *Escanaba*'s horns. The ship sounded very far away now. There was no chance of him catching up to it.

And outside, dark shapes shambled through the night, still moving in the direction of the East River.

"Don't leave," the woman said finally. Gartrell looked back at her and saw she had lowered her weapon. He did the same.

"All right. Stay cool."

Gartrell slowly moved forward and knelt beside her on the cold tile floor. He reached out and put a hand on her shoulder, and she jumped slightly at the contact. Even through his glove, he felt her body was so tense it was almost rigid. She looked toward his face, and she must have seen the vague green glow emanating from the displays of his NVGs. She reached out with her right hand and found his, and to Gartrell's amusement, she shook it quickly.

"I'm Jolie," she said.

"Gartrell. Or Dave, whichever you prefer. Mind if I see your weapon for just a moment?"

She handed it to him wordlessly. It was an old J-frame revolver, more popularly known as a Saturday Night Special, the kind of piece he really only saw in the 1950s detective movies he so loved. He opened the cylinder. It was five-shot weapon of .38 caliber, fully loaded. He closed the cylinder and put the weapon back in her hand.

"Do you know how to shoot that?"

"Yes. My husband insisted I learn, so I did." She paused for a moment. "It's not hard."

"I know. What are you doing down here, Jolie?"

She reached out with her left hand, fumbling in the darkness. Gartrell saw several small paper bags beside her, and he guided her hand to them. She lifted one and handed it to him. Gartrell opened the bag. Inside was a piece of frosted cake. He sniffed it. Lemon cake.

"So you have a thing for Starbucks lemon cake?"

"No. My son does," she said.

Oh hell. "Your son. How old?"

"He's four years old." As she said this, her face was blank, almost expressionless.

Gartrell slowly rose to his feet and looked around the coffee shop. Outside, the arty still blasted away in the distance. Much closer, the sounds of the moaning dead floated on the air.

"Is he here?" Gartrell asked. He cradled his AA-12 in both hands as a stench staggered past outside. Its shoulder rubbed against the pane glass window, leaving a vague trail of ichor behind it.

"No. He's upstairs. Asleep."

"Upstairs where?"

"Our apartment." He looked down at her as she pointed toward the coffee shop's ceiling. "We live on the fourth floor of the building."

Gartrell considered that. The sun would be coming up soon, and his preference was to be above street level when that happened. Things were dicey enough when it was dark out; during the day, the dead would be able to hunt more easily.

"How do we get there?"

She gathered the sacks of cake and stuffed them into a large handbag that hung from her shoulder. She then rose to her feet.

"Follow me," she said.

She started off toward the dining area. Gartrell moved to follow, then checked himself. He went back to the display case and filled two bags with cinnamon coffee cake. He then stuffed water bottles into the cargo pockets on his BDU trousers. Only then did he hurry after the woman as she slowly picked her way through the dark dining area. He couldn't quite figure out where she was going, then he saw it: the long window overlooking the dining area was gone. It lay scattered throughout the dining area in thousands of shards. The glass made crunching, popping noises as they walked across it.

I guess she didn't know the front door was open.

"I used the window because the apartment building is right next door," she said, as if reading his mind. "If I'd tried to use the front door, I would have had to walk around the corner, and those things would have got me."

"You broke the window yourself?"

"No."

She stepped onto a chair and boosted herself onto the window sill. Gartrell was impressed that she was able to step onto it without any kind of handhold, and in total darkness at the same time. He reached out and touched her ankle, preventing her from stepping out of the Starbucks.

"I'll go first," he whispered. She nodded and pulled the revolver from the waistband of her jeans where she'd put it. Her index finger fell upon the trigger guard. Gartrell stepped onto the chair and, mindful of the broken glass, hoisted himself up to join her. He leaned out into the street, moving slowly, cautiously. Shapes moved in the gloom, but he remained undetected. Gartrell motioned Jolie outside, and followed her as she darted to a nearby door. She inserted a key into the lock and twisted it. Gartrell thought the lock disengaged with all the subtlety of a gunshot in a mausoleum, but the noise did not attract any unwanted attention—yet. Jolie pulled open the door and held it for him as he backed inside, keeping his AA-12 oriented toward the street. He caught the door as it closed and gently sealed it with no noise whatsoever. And just in time; a dark shape loomed right outside the glass. Gartrell grabbed Jolie's arm and held her rooted to the spot as the zed lurched against the door and peered inside with milky, stupid eyes. Its mouth was open, and its blackening tongue lolled between a gap in its teeth. Gartrell practically held his breath, his automatic shotgun in both hands, its barrel pointed directly at the ghoul as it looked right at him without seeing him. Gartrell wondered if it would be content to stare into the apartment building's darkened entry hall until the sun rose.

After a time, it finally shambled off into the night.

Guess even they can get bored.

"We should go," Jolie said finally. "Can you let go of my arm? You're squeezing it a bit too hard."

Gartrell did as she asked, and she rubbed her forearm with her hand. She pocketed the key and slipped the revolver back into the waistband of her jeans, then turned toward the hallway behind them. She slowly picked her way to a white door and reached for its brass knob.

"Hold up," Gartrell said.

She stopped with her hand only an inch from the doorknob. "Why?"

"Give me a second." Gartrell looked around the lobby. It was a pre-war building, one of those many structures that had been built before World War II. The lobby had been regentrified, with a granite floor and an ornate ceiling from which hung art deco light fixtures that would remain dark for quite a while longer. A row of mailboxes were set into the wall near the door, across from a desk where the doorman would normally be stationed.

"What's on this floor?" he asked.

"Laundry. Elevators. Stairs. Storage, with more below."

"How many stories?"

"Sixteen."

"And how many people are left in the building?"

"No one. They evacuated." Her face was no longer blank and expressionless. She looked agitated. "Listen, I need to get to my son. You want to look around? Knock yourself out."

"I'm good," Gartrell said.

She pulled open the door, and it led into a stairwell. At the base of the stairs was a long, black Maglite. She picked it up and looked back at him.

"Close the door so I can turn this on."

"Why don't you forget about that for a moment and let me go up first," he said. "You turn that on, my night vision gear will blank out, and it's more useful right now than a flashlight. You get what I'm saying?"

"No."

Gartrell sighed. "The zeds, they can key in on light real well. Not doing things like giving off light, loud noises, probably even smells like cooking food and things like that will go a long way toward ensuring our continued survival. And if there's a zed in this stairway, for instance, it'll see the light long before we see it. You reading me on that now?"

"You don't want me to use the light. You want to use your night vision. Fine. Let's go to the fourth floor. You first."

Gartrell nodded and mounted the steps, taking them one at a time, his AA-12 at the ready. As it always was.

The climb up the stairwell was uneventful, but halfway to the fourth floor, Gartrell's legs felt as if they were Jell-O and his lungs were on fire. He had to fight to keep from gasping for air, and he continued the climb through sheer force of will alone. He couldn't believe how much of a struggle it was just to keep moving; he would have gladly surrendered his kingdom, if he'd had one, for the chance to stop and lean against the wall and rest. His body was sending him a strong reminder that he was well into his late 40s and had been operating at a punishing pace for virtually 24 hours straight. When he slowed to listen for any indication that they might not be alone, all he heard was the rush of blood in his ears.

The only thing that kept him going was that he didn't want to look bad in front of the civilian, who just happened to be a female.

For her part, Jolie followed closely behind. Her footfalls were light, almost as quiet as a cat's, whereas his echoed throughout the stairwell. Gartrell went through the usual motions, visually clearing each landing before stepping onto it, holding the AA-12 so that he could instantly fire on any zed that might appear. But the building remained as quiet as a crypt, and as far as he could tell, they were the only things—living or unliving—in the stairway.

Finally, they arrived on the fourth floor.

Gartrell pushed open the door and cleared the hallway, then reached back and touched Jolie on the shoulder. She slipped past him and walked to the left, her right arm extended, the fingertips of her hand brushing against the wall. Her tennis shoes made no noise on the carpeted floor. Gartrell silently closed the door behind him and followed, keeping to Jolie's left so he could maintain a clear lane of fire. She stopped at a door just down the hall and unlocked its two security deadbolts. The sounds of the locks snapping opening were loud and harsh as they echoed in the hallway. Gartrell winced at the racket, but they elicited nothing untoward. The door squeaked minutely as she pushed it open. Light flared, threatening to overpower the NVGs—there must have been a small nightlight switched on somewhere inside the apartment. Gartrell followed her inside and took note of the number on the door: 4B.

She closed the door behind him and held a finger to her lips. Gartrell nodded, and flipped his NVGs up on their mount. Without the goggles, the darkness inside the apartment was almost absolute; he had no natural night vision to speak of since he'd spent the last few hours staring at the phosphor screens inside the NVG tubes. He removed his gloves and rubbed his eyes. They burned, from weariness and exposure to smoke and the heat of roaring flame. When he stopped and looked up, Jolie was gone. Gartrell stood there for a moment, waiting for his eyes to adjust to the tepid light. He locked the door behind him, and then flicked on the security chain for good measure. The door was painted metal, a fire door fitted inside a metal frame, but the hinges looked flimsy, the kind a cheap contractor would use. He turned away from the door and found he stood in a short entry foyer with closets off to either side. He walked down the short hallway. Dim light came from a doorway on his right. He looked inside, and saw the room beyond was a kitchen illuminated by a single, battery-powered LED light sitting on a dark silestone counter. Stainless steel appliances gleamed in the wan glow. Gartrell worried the light might be visible from outside, but not only had the shades been drawn, but paper was taped over the shades' edges. Moving on down the hallway, he came to a return which led him to a darkened combination living and dining room. An expensive-looking widescreen LED television framed in what Gartrell thought was rosewood stood atop an equally-expensive media table. A surround sound system's speakers were placed strategically through the room. Gartrell moved toward one and squinted to read its product label in the light generated by another tiny LED lamp sitting on a nearby bookshelf. Polk Audio.

Fine stuff.

A leather seating set was arrayed before the television. Next to the TV was a fireplace, though Gartrell couldn't tell if it was real or one of those faux decorative touches he'd heard a lot of New Yorkers favored. Several pictures hung on the wall, and he leaned forward to examine them. Jolie was in many, though most featured a small boy with a distant expression. A man he presumed to be the boy's father was in several photos as well. He looked to be in his 30s, and something of a cross between a hipster and a finance guy, with his expensive-looking business attire, skimpy beard, and artfully messed-up hair. He apparently dabbled in local politics as well, for there were several photos of him with political figures—all Democrats, of course. There was even one of him mugging it up with a ranking member of the U.S. Senate, a very liberal New York Democrat who was totally anti-war until the current president needed to show the nation how tough he was. Whenever that happened, the senator never met a conflict he didn't like.

One ceramic frame held a family portrait. Names were written on the frame: *Jack, Jolie, and Jaden.*

Gartrell snorted. *A family where all the names begin with the letter J. I guess I really am on New York's Upper East Side.*

A few works of art occupied high shelves in a display case—bronze statues, knickknacks from different countries, a framed coin collection. The lower shelves were filled with the trappings one might expect to find in a residence where a small child lived. Bright, smiling cartoon characters, toy trucks and airplanes and boats, building blocks, a small riding scooter. The dining area was a round table surrounded by four chairs; there were no place settings, and the table was covered with canned goods and other items—plastic trash bags, paper towels, bottled water and juice, a bucket full of cleaning supplies. Two North Face backpacks sat on the Persian rug beneath the table, packs that were probably more expensive than the one he had left in the white van the team had driven cross-town in their gamble to reach the East River and the cutter *Escanaba*. The packs were likely more comfortable, as well. Gartrell didn't inspect them any further. He walked toward one of the shaded windows and stood next to it, listening.

The artillery barrage to the north continued unabated, a distant earthquake that went on forever. There was no other sound he could detect, no moaning dead, no wind, no distant horn blasts from the *Escanaba*—

Movement in the darkness caused him to spin away from the window, and the AA-12 fell into its normal firing position on complete reflex. Jolie looked at him from across the room, her eyes—blue eyes, he thought, but the light was so dim he couldn't be sure—narrowed in what he took to be consternation. Gartrell slowly relaxed and for the first time he could remember, he took his finger off the AA-12's trigger.

"Sorry about that," he muttered.

She waved him to silence with one strident motion. There were two doors behind her, one on either side of the fireplace and media station. Gartrell presumed one led to the child's bedroom, while the other led to the parents'. Jolie stalked past him and beckoned for him to follow. Gartrell trailed after her as she led him into the kitchen, where she picked up the small LED lamp and turned down a short, dark hallway he had missed before, right past the refrigerator. She slid open a pocket door at the end of the hall and stepped into the room beyond. Gartrell followed, stepping lightly across the polished ceramic tile floor.

The room was quite small, barely worthy of being called a guest room. It contained a twin bed, a miniscule closet, and a small bureau. A narrow door led to what he presumed was a bathroom. The single strip window there was blacked out like the rest.

"You have to be quiet," she said after she closed the pocket door behind them. They stood almost cheek-to-cheek at the foot of the bed, which took up almost all the available room. "My son is on a very regular schedule. I can't have it interrupted, do you understand?"

"A 'regular schedule'?" Gartrell couldn't quite believe his ears. "Look ma'am, it's not like he's going to be able to get up and watch cartoons tomorrow morning before he goes off to school, you know what I mean?"

Jolie shook her head sharply. "No. You don't get it. My son is autistic. Variations in his schedule make him act out. Yelling. Screaming. I can't have that right now. Not when those things might hear him. Do you understand now?"

"Ah...okay." Gartrell sighed at the revelation, and a small part of him suddenly regretted linking up with this woman, even though she offered him the chance to find at least partial shelter from the storm of dead meat stalking the streets of the Upper East Side. And he was no stranger to autism; one of his brothers had a son who was moderately autistic, and he also exhibited a very limited ability to process new experiences before breaking down and becoming so disorganized he could hardly walk.

"I get what you mean about the autism," he told Jolie. "Whereabouts on the spectrum is he? Asperger's, or—"

"Classical autism. He doesn't speak, doesn't point, and has difficulty controlling himself and understanding requests." She paused. "And he wouldn't understand that we're all in danger. That's why I need to pay as close attention to his routine as possible. You understand?"

Gartrell nodded. He understood, and the more he knew about it, the less he liked it.

Hang tough, old dog. These are the cards you've been dealt.

"Why didn't you evacuate?" he asked.

"My husband and I agreed we would wait for him, so we could leave together. I was afraid I might get separated from Jaden if I tried to take him out of the city alone."

"I take it your husband never made it home."

"He…he was coming from downtown. He was in the quarantine area in the Financial District. When he tried to leave, he…he couldn't get out right away, but they were going to try and make it past the police blockades. When he called me last before the cell phones went out, they had made it all the way up to Thirteenth Street. But…" Jolie looked past him and seemed to shrug, her eyes (*They* are *blue*, Gartrell thought) distant and haunted. "But he never came. And by the time I got things together enough to try and make a break for it, it was too late. *They* were already in the streets." She nodded toward the window behind Gartrell. "They killed the police at the corner barricade. I could hear the fighting and…and the screaming."

"You should have left with everyone else," Gartrell said. "Your neighbors, other family…they could have helped with your boy."

"You don't understand. We never really knew our neighbors, though the Skinners next door tried to get me to go with them. And our friends…well, they had families of their own to take care of." Jolie looked up at him after a moment. "What happened to you? Where are the rest of your soldiers?"

"Dead, mostly. Some…the officer I was supporting and some civilians made it to a Coast Guard cutter in the East River. I was cut off." He waved the question away. "Anyway, it's not important now. When does your son normally wake up? It'll be daylight soon."

"Seven-thirty. Sometimes eight, eight-thirty."

Gartrell checked his watch. It was 4:18am. "Roger that. All right, you should get some sleep. We're going to have our hands full with him tomorrow. How do you think he'll respond to me being here?"

"I don't know."

"Well, we'll have to do the best we can. Will you sleep with him? In his room?"

"Yes."

"You have to make sure he doesn't pull the shades off the windows," Gartrell said. "If those things in the street see him, they'll know where we are. They're plenty stupid, but when there's food on the table, there are enough of them to make a difference in how things will go down. Understand?"

"I know. Like I said, they killed the police manning the barricades on Second Avenue."

"My team and I were in a fortified high rise building, and they broke into it and took it down. We barely got out. Listen, ninety-nine percent of those stenches out there are as stupid as a bag of rocks—but a few of them are smart enough to figure out things like doors and the like, you understand? They see us in here, from the street or from maybe another building, they'll try and get to us. And there's no way to reason with these things. The only thing they understand is that they want to eat—nothing else matters. Nothing. No negotiation, no chance for last-minute mercy, *nothing*. They see us, we have to boogie, and real, real quick."

"Where would we go?"

Gartrell sighed and rubbed his eyes tiredly. "I don't know. I need to figure that one out. You're sure none of your neighbors are around?"

"No. They all left, like I said. I've been all through the building—most of the apartments are locked, but I've been in a few that aren't, and no one's around. That's where I got all the stuff on the dining room table."

"I noticed that. Good, so you've already scavenged a lot of stuff. How many apartments are on each floor?"

"Two."

"Have you been in the apartment next door?"

"No. The Skinners locked up when they left. Why?"

"Because we'll need a place to fall back to in case this unit gets compromised."

She looked at him oddly. "Like I said…it's locked. We can't 'fall back' to it, unless you want to break down the door. And what good would it be then?"

Gartrell waved the question away. "We'll go over that tomorrow. For now, though…we ought to get some sleep. We might be here for a while, so we should take the opportunity to rest while we can. Can I bunk in here?"

Jolie nodded. "Sure."

"Great. Thanks."

"I'll catch you tomorrow morning, then."

She left, taking the LED light with her. Gartrell closed the door, then reached behind him and felt around for the bed. It was right behind him, and he slowly lowered himself onto it. The mattress was firm, just how he liked it. He stretched out on it and found it wasn't lumpy at all—an extra bonus. He stood the AA-12 on its butt stock in the corner, between the bed and the wall, figuring it would be relatively safe from a certain young boy's inquisitive fingers, at least as long as he was in the room. He flipped on the radio and scrolled through the frequencies. The ones assigned to the former OMEN Team were silent, as he had expected. He tried to raise McDaniels, but he was certain the major was well out of range as the Coast Guard cutter returned to the open Atlantic Ocean. The rest of the open frequencies were mostly silent, devoid of any organized chatter, though a few of them did reveal some garbled transmissions. Gartrell identified himself and tried to make contact, but no one responded to his calls.

Exhaustion hit him suddenly, and Gartrell slowly pulled off the remainders of his gear. His web belt and his MP5 went under the bed, while the radio and knapsack and the contents of his pockets went on the bureau. He would take a full inventory of his meager possessions when the sun came up. But for now, he needed as much sleep as he could get. He stretched out on the bed fully clothed and stared into the blackness, listening to the sounds of the building and the city beyond. The artillery continued exploding in the distance. Gartrell figured the 10th Mountain Division or whoever was launching the attack was going for pure neutralization fire. He hoped the arty would be effective against the zeds, but knowing them as he did, he rather doubted it.

And with that cheery thought in his head, Gartrell fell into a deep, dreamless sleep.

When he awoke, it was daytime.

At first, he couldn't remember where he was. He looked about the small bedroom, blinking against the dim light that filtered past the window shade. He saw his gear lying on the bureau next to his head—his radio, his web belt, the grenades, magazines of ammunition, his knapsack, flares, bottled water, white plastic quick ties, paper bags with the Starbucks logo on them—and wondered how it all got there. Then he remembered the woman from the night before, the one he had met in the blacked-out Starbucks, the one who had been prowling through the store looking for lemon cake. He sat up in the bed and listened, but the apartment was quiet. He checked his watch. 9:37am. As Gartrell swung his legs over the edge of the bed, he was struck by something else.

The artillery barrage had stopped.

That could have happened for several reasons, one of them being the arty emplacements had been overrun by the walking dead. Or they had run out of ammunition. Or the advancing echelons of the dead had been destroyed, though he thought that unlikely. Or the artillery batteries were repositioning, or had ceased fire so other units could move in and secure the zone…

Enough guessing. Let's see what we can find out.

He donned his radio headset and switched on the transceiver. He scanned through the channels, and was overjoyed to discover several frequencies had become operational. He announced himself on them using his mission call sign, but he received no response on the first two frequencies he tried.

The third time was the charm, however. On another frequency, he captured someone's attention.

"Call sign Terminator Five, this is Summit Three-Seven. Say again, over."

"Summit Three-Seven, this is Terminator Five. I'm solo in New York City after a busted mission on the Upper East Side. What's the situation in the world? Over."

"Terminator Five, this is Summit Three-Seven, a command and control element with the two-eight-seven infantry. This is an operational frequency for the Summit battalion. You sure you're in the right place? Over."

"Summit Three-Seven, Terminator Five. I was part of an alpha detachment that went tango uniform about twenty-four hours ago. My frequencies are dead, because there are no other SOF units in the zone. Looks like you lightfighters are all I've got. If you have another frequency I can roll to, give it to me and I'll give it a shot, over."

Another voice came over the radio. "Terminator, this is Summit Six. Give me your name and unit, over."

Gartrell's spirits rose slightly. He was now speaking to the commander of the Summit Battalion, which he knew to be the Second Battalion, 87th Infantry, a tenant unit of Fort Drum and part of the 10th Mountain Division. The infantry battalion CO would be lieutenant colonel, maybe someone with enough horsepower to get something done about his situation.

"First Sergeant David Gartrell, current senior NCO, Echo Company, First Battalion, First Special Warfare Training Group at the Swick. Was pulled out of my normal duty position and assigned to Operational Detachment Alpha OMEN on an emergency basis, over." Before deploying into the field with Major Cordell McDaniels, Gartrell had been a trainer of Special Forces soldiers, posted at the John F. Kennedy Special Warfare Center and School, Fort Bragg, North Carolina. For ease of communication among peers, the name had been shortened to simply SWCS, or more informally, 'Swick'.

"Terminator, Summit Six. You say you're a trainer at the Swick, that correct? How'd a trainer get into the field? Over."

"Summit, Terminator. Long story, Six. But here I am, and I'm wondering if you guys might be able to give me a hand, over."

"Terminator, this is Summit Six. Listen, we have our hands pretty full at the moment. I'll try and find a Special Forces liaison to talk this over with, but we have several synchronized movement to contact ops underway right now. You probably know better than we do, but these things are damned hard to kill, over."

"Summit, Terminator. You got that wrong, Six, they're *easy* to kill—you just have to hit them in the head to put them down for the count. Nothing else works, not even major deboning injuries, unless you blast them to pieces. And listen, you need to watch out for something. Ninety-nine percent of those things are brainless, but some of them can come back with skills. We were shagged by members of our own ODA, and they still knew how to use guns and get their stalk on. Let me know if you got that. Over."

There was a long moment of silence, and then the infantry commander came back on the air. "Uh, Terminator Five, this is Summit Six. Understand you just said that some of the zeds can conduct...coordinated offensive operations, is that correct? Over."

"Summit, Terminator. Roger that, you are correct. Certain zeds can retain pre-existing high-level skills, though they are not one hundred percent mission capable. But they *can* operate weapons and machinery—we had stenches roll up on us in a taxi cab and open up with assault rifles. I would advise you to make the appropriate notifications. Over."

Summit Six didn't sound thrilled at the prospect. "Roger that last, Terminator."

"Summit, what can you do to help me out here? Terminator's single gun with two civilian noncombatants, and it feels like we're in the middle of stench city. Do you have any aviation assets you can send my way? Over."

"Terminator, Summit. Negative, we have zero airlift, only attack. All our transport assets were surged down to participate in the evacuation op you must have been part of. We're trying to get into Central Park to recover some airframes, but that's going to take a while." Gartrell grunted to himself as Summit Six spoke. He knew all too well that dozens of helicopters, from small scouts to massive medium lift helicopters that could carry upwards of 50 troops were on the deck in Central Park. The assembly area had been overrun by stenches that had broken through the various cordon sanitaires set up throughout the city. It had been obvious then that the military brass calling the shots had underestimated the sheer mass the horde could bring to bear.

"How long can you hold out at your current pos, Terminator? Over."

Gartrell rose and walked to the window. He slowly peeled back some of the tape that held the window shade in place and peered out into the bright day, squinting against the harsh sunlight. The street outside—Second Avenue—was full of abandoned cars. At the corner nearby, where East 86th Street intersected with the broad avenue, a roadblock had been set up with New York City snow plows. It had been overrun a day ago, and judging by the amount of brass cartridges that twinkled in the sunlight, it had been some fight. The rains of the preceding night had washed away most of the blood, but Gartrell saw strips of cloth, shoes and boots, and fallen weapons lying on the street.

And of course, the zombies were everywhere. Hundreds of them. Most milled about aimlessly, waiting for some clue as to where their next meal might be. They shambled about like automatons, moving between the vehicles in the traffic-choked street. Most kept their eyes down low, looking for food at ground level. But not all. Though they couldn't see Gartrell through the small opening he peered through, some of the stenches below scanned the buildings from the street, actively searching the windows for signs of prey. Gartrell taped the window shade back in place, and gloom returned to the tiny bedroom.

"Summit, this is Terminator. If the zeds get a lock on us, we'll be lucky to have ten minutes. Over."

"Roger that, Terminator. I need to park you on another frequency. I've got battalion-level reports coming my way in just a couple of minutes. Stand by, over."

"Roger Six, I'll stand by here. Over."

During the pause, Gartrell opened one of the water bottles he'd taken from the Starbucks downstairs. He was parched as all hell, and he drank from the bottle with gusto. His growling stomach informed him some chow would be a great idea as well. He consumed one of the cinnamon coffee cakes in virtually three bites. It was stale, but he barely noticed.

Even stale coffee cake is better than an MRE.

"Terminator Five, Summit Six. Over."

"Summit, this is Terminator, go ahead. Over."

"Terminator, I've got a place to park you for the moment." The infantry commander on the other end of the radio link read off a frequency. Gartrell pulled out his pen and wrote the freq on the brown Starbucks bag on the bureau before him. "Can you make that frequency? Over."

"Summit, Terminator. Roger, I can make that frequency. Over."

"Roger that, Terminator. Switch over now. Summit out." As Summit Six finished his sentence, another transmission began, and Gartrell heard the terror in the reporting soldier's voice. He was in contact with the horde, and the engagement wasn't getting any better with age. Gartrell didn't bother to acknowledge Summit Six's transmission, for another report came in, stomping over the first one. Summit Six wouldn't be able to hear him anyway, and it sounded like the light infantry battalion commander had more pressing things on his plate right now.

Gartrell switched over to the allocated frequency and announced himself. He heard only the slight hiss of background static, marred every now and then with some bleed-over from a neighboring frequency. He couldn't make out the contents of the radio traffic, as the distortion level was extremely high. It could have been anything—more lightfighters in contact and looking for help, probably. Or maybe something as mundane as a truck convoy looking for directions.

"Terminator Five, this is Falcon Four, over."

"Falcon, this is Terminator, go ahead."

"Terminator, Falcon. I understand you're caught behind the lines in the Upper East Side, is that correct? Over."

"Falcon, Terminator. That is a roger, over."

"Terminator, this is Falcon. Did Summit Six notify you that most of our elements are either in contact with the zeds, or soon will be? We're a little stretched for resources right now. Over."

"Falcon, that kind of came up in the conversation right after I asked for help, over."

"Uh…got that, Terminator. Listen, we need you to stay tight. We're looking for a way to get to you, but with all the north-south routes basically blocked with dead traffic, our guys can't get in with vehicles. They have to hoof it. It's going to take a long time, and they'll have to fight from block to block, over."

Gartrell buried his face in his hands. *What the hell are they thinking? Of course they can't take any vehicles in!*

"Falcon, Terminator. I know I'm not in your command silo, but I'm Special Forces and I've been behind the line of troops for more than a day. These things do not give up. They will not stop. Sending dismounted troops at them is only going to embolden the zeds and get your guys killed. You can't treat this as a normal movement-to-contact mission, the zeds have no ability to be afraid of your firepower, and they will swarm over each unit you send in until they defeat it by mass of bodies alone. This is a no-shit assessment from a guy who's been there, done that. Over."

"Roger Terminator, I get that. I'll—I'll advise Six of that as soon as I can. He's a little busy right now, over."

"Falcon, Terminator. He's busy getting his guys killed. You'd better grow a pair and tap that guy on the shoulder right now, otherwise the only thing that'll be left of his battalion is the headquarters company. You read me? Over."

"I read you, Terminator." Falcon didn't seem to grasp the urgency of the situation, which left Gartrell incensed. If the entire 10th Mountain Division was fed to the zeds, then there wasn't going to be anyone left to help him out.

"Falcon, Terminator. What's your position in the Two-Eight-Seven, over?"

"Terminator, Falcon...say again? Over."

"Falcon. This is Terminator." Gartrell had a tough time keeping the frustration out of his voice. "I asked what your duty station was. Are you with the S-Three shop? S-Two? What?"

"Terminator, this is Falcon. I'm...I'm with the battalion S-Five, over."

Gartrell was dumbfounded. "Falcon...you're with the battalion's *public relations* shop?"

"Uh...roger that, Terminator. Like I said, we're a bit pressed for resources right at the moment—"

"Falcon, this is Terminator. Stay on this frequency. I'll come back to you in one second." Gartrell flipped back to the 2/87th's common net, and found it was saturated with radio traffic from infantry units that were in contact with the legion of the dead. It was horrifying to listen to, but Gartrell had unfortunately heard it all before.

"Summit Six, this is Terminator Five! Pull your troops back, don't push them into the zeds! Pull your troops back, or they're gone, over!"

A half-dozen transmissions stomped on his as he tried to speak. He repeated the transmission several times, but he wasn't getting through. The net was jammed. He was about to roll back to the frequency Falcon was waiting on, but a voice caught his attention.

"Terminator! Terminator, this is Yankee Five-Five-Six! We're pinned down at the intersections of First Avenue and One Twenty-Seventh, you have anything you can help us with? The fucking zeds, they're all over the place! Over!"

"Yankee Five-Five-Six, Terminator's got nothing for you. You need to fall back or fortify your position, over." Again, Gartrell's transmission was stomped on mercilessly. He didn't know New York City very well, but the Yankee unit's position put it on the Harlem side of the East River—or was it called the Harlem River up there? Whichever, it didn't matter. What it *did* mean is that the stenches had rolled all the way through Manhattan and Harlem throughout the night, which meant the Bronx would be the next borough to go. And as tough as he'd heard folks were in the South Bronx, he was pretty sure they wouldn't hold up for very long against thousands of walking, flesh-eating corpses.

He repeated the advice to Yankee 556 twice more, but he heard nothing further from the unit. He caught snatches of conversation between other units and their commanders on the frequency, and the overall impression he got while listening to their fragmented reports was essentially grim. The lightfighters weren't just getting their asses kicked, they were getting them bitten off. With a sigh, he rolled back to the frequency Falcon waited on.

"Falcon, Terminator. Give me a read on your side, over."

"Terminator, this is Summit Six. I told you stay on this channel!"

Gartrell was surprised to hear the infantry commander's voice on the radio. "Sorry Six, I could have sworn when I'd left there was just a PAO weenie on this frequency. If I'd known you were coming over, I wouldn't have switched back to try and get you on the command net. Over."

"Terminator, I don't have a lot of time. My troops are getting slaughtered over there, and some of them are cut off. Falcon tells me you may have some guidance. Over."

My, my, my. When Big Army gets its panties in a bunch, who does it call? The snake-eaters, of course. "Your troops need to stay organized, practice fire discipline, and get to cover, Six. They're in a vertical urban environment, the only place to go is up—they'll have to try and gain access to buildings and fortify in-place." Something tickled the back of Gartrell's mind, and he reached for it. "Uh, that's not all, Six. They can go down, into the subway tunnels. Zed can't see in the dark, so if your troops have night vision, they can use that to their advantage. Over."

"Terminator, Summit—if they go underground, we'll lose commo with them. That's a non-starter, over."

"Six, you want your troops coming back to you alive? If not, they'll come back to you dead, and some of them might still remember how to use their guns. It is what it is, Six. Get 'em underground and save some of them, or lose them all. Over."

Summit Six's voice was grim. "Roger that, Terminator. Thanks for the assist. We'll see what we can do about getting you some transport out of there. Falcon will remain on this frequency. Summit Six, out." The infantry commander disappeared from the radio before Gartrell could reply.

How rude, he thought.

"Ah, Terminator, this is Falcon Four, over."

"Go ahead, Falcon."

"Terminator, Falcon…look, thanks for trying to help our guys out. I hear the colonel now, he's ordering everyone to either fall back or get into the subway tunnels if they can. It sounds like it's probably their only chance, and no one here was even thinking that way before you brought it up. Over."

"Falcon, if you're trying to cheer me up by painting me was a genius among idiots, do note that I'm currently depending on those same idiots to save my ass, along with the two civilians I'm trapped behind the lines with. Over."

"Roger that, Terminator."

"Falcon, Terminator. Can you give me a run-down on what's been happening over the past twenty-four hours or so? I've been a bit out of the loop, and Terminator Six took the sat phone so I haven't exactly been able to keep tabs on current events. Over."

There was a long pause before Falcon came back. "Terminator, this is Falcon. I don't know how much I can tell you, but things aren't improving. We're trying to contain New

York City, but there are outbreaks happening all over the country. Mostly on the East Coast, I think. Florida, DC, the Carolinas, Maryland, New Jersey…seems like wherever there's a major seaport, these things are getting in. Homeland Security is trying to lock down the coastline, but that's not really happening. All airspace has been sanitized for the past eighteen hours after a plane landed in Chicago with zeds on it. Don't know much about the West Coast, but things have been pretty quiet over there. Over."

"Falcon, Terminator. What about Europe? Over."

"Ah…Terminator, I'm not sure. Russia's gone dark, and a lot of Eastern Europe too. Germany and France are fighting zeds in their own countries. Seems like Britain and Switzerland are still hanging tough, along with the northern European countries, but beyond that, I don't really know. The BBC was still broadcasting last I knew, but I haven't been able to check into that lately." There was another pause. "Sorry man, the questions you're asking are way above my pay grade right now. Over."

Gartrell digested that for a long moment. The news, while not unexpected, was still chilling. Was the United States falling before a…a zombie apocalypse, like in the movie *Dawn of the Dead*?

Jesus, what about Laurie and the kids? Is the cabin remote enough? Can they get to it? Can they defend it?

"Terminator, you still there? Over."

Gartrell pushed the thoughts of his family away for the moment. "Roger that, Falcon. Terminator's still here. Listen, when do you think you might be able to report back on an extraction? I'm here with a mother and a special needs child. If things go to hell, I'm going to be in a pretty tough spot. Over."

"Terminator, Falcon. Roger that, I get what you're saying. We're going to do our very best, but for the time being, you'd better just lay low. Over."

"Falcon, listen to me. I've been in this position just a few hours ago, and we had a fortified location with enough food and water to last for weeks. We had several Special Forces hooahs and troops from the 160 SOAR to keep the goblins at bay, and we still got pushed out. These things, they can bring a hell of a lot of mass to bear. I'm in a fourth floor apartment, man. If these things decide they want to come up and see what's on the menu, the only thing that's standing between the stenches and a kid and his mother is me, and I've got about ten seconds of combat time before I'm weapons dry. I don't mean to sound like my mascara is starting to run, but you get what I'm saying here? Over."

"Roger that, Terminator. Get what you're saying a hundred percent. But I'm telling you the truth, we don't have the assets to get you out just yet. I've heard there are some Chinooks spooling up from a Pennsylvania National Guard unit—other 'Hook units from Connecticut and upstate New York are standing up now. Those are your best shot, but they're not here yet. As soon as they come in, we'll send something your way. Even sooner if another unit makes it on site, but for now, you have to wait. Over." Falcon sounded sincere enough, but Gartrell knew the man was just a public affairs officer. How much horsepower could he possibly have? Even though PAOs were part of the Army structure, Gartrell had very little faith in a media wrangler whose only job was to blow sunshine through innocuous press releases.

"Falcon, this is Terminator. Roger your last. We'll keep our heads down and do the best we can until we can get some support. What do you recommend for a contact schedule? Over."

"Terminator, Falcon Four. Let's talk in sixty minutes, hooah?"

"Roger Falcon, sixty minutes. Terminator Five, out."

Gartrell slowly removed his radio headset and rubbed his eyes. Despite having fallen into a dreamless sleep, he still felt exhausted. And his body ached—all his joints were stiff and sore, and his thigh muscles twitched and burned. He forced himself to his feet and walked into the microscopic bathroom that adjoined the bedroom. A shower stall was to his left. To his right was the toilet, and dead ahead was a small sink with a medicine cabinet. He looked at his face in the mirror there, and was surprised to see just how haggard and run-down he looked. His cheeks, chin, and neck were covered with blond-brown razor stubble that was sprinkled liberally with gray. The creases in his forehead and the wrinkles around his dark eyes and mouth seemed as deep as canyons. The skin beneath his eyes was puffy, and dirt marred his features, serving only to exacerbate his overall unhealthy look. He looked at his hands. They were covered with grime, as was his uniform. First Sergeant David Gartrell definitely looked like a troop who had been to hell and back again.

And to think it's only starting.

He opened the medicine cabinet. Inside was a box of cotton balls, rubbing alcohol, hydrogen peroxide, a tiny bottle of Tylenol that expired almost a year ago. He opened it and dry-swallowed two of the caplets inside, then turned to the toilet. After he lifted the lid and undid his trousers, he hesitated for a moment. The water in the toilet bowl was clear and clean. Water might soon become a precious resource. He turned and pissed into the sink instead, and listened to his urine wind its way down the drain. He was certain the lady of the house would disapprove of his measures, but if she ever discovered his transgression and made to complain, he would remind her of his foresight should it ever come to pass they needed the water in the toilet bowl. Just the same, when he was finished he opened the sink faucet. A small stream of water trickled out before the pipe started burping air, and he turned it off quickly. At least enough water had run down the drain to reduce the smell of his urine.

And it's the small pleasures I take comfort in, he thought.

He then inventoried his gear.

The rest of the apartment was dark and gloomy with the shades drawn. Gartrell stepped quietly into the kitchen and took a quick inventory of the items out in plain view. Ignoring the usual fixtures—microwave, toaster, coffee maker (*God, some Joe would taste fucking awesome right now*, he thought), other kitchen appliances—he saw there were bags of chips, half a case of bottled water, four two-liter bottles of Pepsi, a box of cookies, half a loaf of Martin's potato bread. He smelled something rank and sour coming from the stainless steel waste can standing near the doorway to the dining room. It was the stench of feces, still odious beneath a liberal dose of Lysol. He wrinkled his nose in disgust and slowly walked into the dining room.

Jolie was on her knees before a small boy with hair the color of russet that made Gartrell think of copper. Jolie looked over at Gartrell as he stood in the doorway. Her red hair hung in her face as she pulled up the boy's jeans and buttoned them. She still wore the clothes from the night before. Her face was pale, drawn, and her gaze was uneasy. The boy turned to him as well. He was absolutely beautiful, that kind of beauty that only small children seemed to have, completely unsullied, almost angelic. His skin was fair, like his mother's, and totally unblemished. His blue eyes widened when he saw Gartrell, and he took a step toward his mother and put a hand on her cheek. He made a small mewling sound in the back of this throat, and Gartrell watched his beautiful expression become marred by the onslaught of sudden fear.

Gartrell slowly leaned forward and smiled as gently as he could, ignoring his protesting knees and back. He knew he looked like hell, and he didn't blame the kid for being scared. Hell, he was only a few steps away from having Hershey squirts in his drawers himself.

"Hey there," Gartrell said, his voice low and friendly, a tone he didn't have much occasion to use outside of his family. "How're you doing, little guy?" He didn't move any closer, and kept the silly smile on his face. He had only one chance to make a passing impression, and he didn't want to blow it. There was no telling how long the three of them would be cooped up together, and if most of that time could be spent without the boy screaming and yelling in terror because a strange man was in the apartment, Gartrell was ready to move heaven and earth to make it happen.

"His name's Jaden," Jolie said.

"Hiya, Jaden. I'm Dave, and I'm very happy to meet you." Gartrell kept a bouncy, bubbly tone in his voice.

Jaden moaned again and pushed himself into his mother's arms, his face pressed against her shoulder. She smiled and hugged him against her, whispering into his ear. The boy did not cry, but he held onto her for dear life. His small body shook.

"Do you want me to go back into the bedroom?" Gartrell asked.

Jolie shook her head and continued whispering to Jaden, rubbing his back as she planted small kisses on his head. Gartrell straightened up and watched them in the gloomy living room. From the corner of his eye, he saw the goods piled up on the dining room table. He stepped toward it silently and took a quick inventory. More water. Batteries, of all sizes. Cleaning supplies, and Gartrell wondered idly if things such as oven cleaner could somehow be used as a weapon. Bottled juices. Boxes of bandages, over-the-counter medications, and someone's Oxycontin prescription. A box of shotgun shells, which brightened Gartrell's day until he saw they were .410 caliber, far too small to be used in his AA-12. Paper towels, toilet paper, paper napkins. A bag of apples, still hard to his touch. Three containers of wet naps. Gartrell opened one and used several sheets to clean his hands, then ran a few over his face for good measure. The moist, white towelettes were almost completely black by the time he finished.

When he looked up from his work, he saw both Jolie and Jaden were watching him from the living room. Gartrell smiled at the boy, and this time Jaden didn't look away. He made good eye contact with him, and Gartrell knew that was a good sign.

"You look more human now with some of that grime scrubbed away," Jolie said.

Gartrell felt suddenly self-conscious. "Well. I really don't clean up all that well, but I guess anything's an improvement. I'm sorry if I interrupted you, and I'm sorry I frightened Jaden."

"It's okay. It was going to have to happen sooner or later. I want him to see you, so he gets used to you. It's probably better to have it happen now, while there's still some light."

Gartrell nodded, and he smiled at the boy again. Jaden only stared back, his face impassive. He studied Gartrell for several long moments, then slowly turned away and reached for a plastic Sippy cup equipped with a straw. He put the straw in his mouth and took a long drink, his gaze back on Gartrell.

"So he can't speak?" Gartrell asked.

Jolie shook her head. "Only a few words. No real sentences yet. He goes to a special needs preschool on Second and Sixty-Eighth, but school's obviously out now." She ran her fingers through Jaden's hair, brushing it into place. "He loved it there. He was starting to make friends with some of the other children, and they had children there without disabilities, so he could interact with them. He came a long, long way in less than a year."

"He's beautiful," Gartrell said.

"Yes. He is." She reached out and gently grabbed Jaden's chin in her hand and turned his face toward hers. She kissed his forehead and looked into his eyes. "Say hello to—Dave, you said your name was?"

"Yeah. Dave Gartrell."

"Say hello to Dave, sweetie."

Jaden only sucked on his straw and slowly looked back at Gartrell. Gartrell winked at him again, and this time he was rewarded with a tiny shy smile from Jaden as he continued to drink his water. Gartrell's smile broadened.

"A little smile like that is all the hello I need," he said.

Jolie nodded without smiling herself and turned toward the coffee table. A small DVD player sat there, and Gartrell watched as she opened it and turned it on. Its screen came to life, and he felt a twinge of unease run through him.

"Hey, if that thing makes any sound—"

"I'll keep the volume low," Jolie said, her tone harsh. "I have to keep him occupied. If he's unoccupied, he'll start doing things that will cause more noise than a damned DVD, all right?" Jaden made a small noise in his throat when he heard his mother's tone of voice, and Jolie turned back to him, all smiles. She touched his cheek and then tweaked his nose. "We're going to watch some *Blue's Clues*, okay buddy?"

Jaden pulled the straw from his mouth and said, "Boos!" His voice was small but as lovely as he was. Gartrell thought it was a 100% match, and then wondered what it would sound like when the boy broke down and starting wailing. The DVD player's screen came to life with an animated menu, and Jolie selected the 'Play All' icon. The DVD began playing softly, and Jaden giggled a bit as he sat down before it. He stared at the screen with rapt attention, his Sippy cup hanging from his mouth by its straw. Jolie kissed the top of his head again, then picked up a soiled diaper lying on the floor next to her. She rose to her feet and carried the diaper into the kitchen. Gartrell followed, and watched as she put the diaper in a plastic shopping bag, tied it up, and dropped it into the almost-full trash can.

"Jaden's not potty trained yet," she told him. "So we go through quite a few diapers during the day, and a few more overnight. I'm sorry about the smell, but I've been afraid to go out and dump the bag down the garbage chute. I don't know what might hear the noise."

Gartrell nodded. "I get that. You're thinking, and that's good. If the smell gets too bad, we can always pitch the bag into another apartment."

"Who were you talking to before?"

"I made radio contact with the Army unit that's to our north. It's an entire division, maybe ten thousand guys. They're trying to move into the city, but it's not going too well."

"Will they come and get us?"

"As soon as they can. They're a little short on helicopters right now, but they know we're here. By the way, I'll need your address—I can give them GPS information, but an actual address would help."

"Fifteen-forty Second Avenue, apartment four B. When do you think they'll come?"

Gartrell shrugged. "Not sure—they're waiting for helicopters to come in from Pennsylvania. I don't know if they've left their home airfield yet, or if they're even ready to launch. I'll make contact again in an hour and try to get an update, but lots of stuff is going on in the world. We're pretty low on the list of priorities right now."

Jolie's brow knitted. "Did you tell them I have an autistic son?"

"I mentioned that, yeah. Look, they're going to try, but they're also trying to stop those…things…from getting out of the city. You know what happens if one bites you, right?"

"No. What?"

Gartrell sighed. "You die. And then, you turn into one of them."

Jolie stared at him for a long moment, then looked away. "Dear sweet Jesus." She put her hands over her face. "Oh dear sweet *Jesus*, you mean—" Her voice broke and her shoulders shook as she sobbed. She tried to suppress it, but the emotion overwhelmed her. She wept as silently as she could, and Gartrell stepped toward her and put his hands on her shoulders.

"What's wrong? Have you been bitten? Are you all right?"

She shook her head and pulled away from him. He let her, and stepped back so he could keep an eye on Jaden. The boy still sat in front of the DVD player, watching a cute animated dog named Blue cavort about with her human owner. Gartrell looked back at Jolie, and waited for her to get herself under control.

"What is it, ma'am? If you've got something to say, pull yourself together and say it."

She reached for a roll of paper towels and tore off a sheet. She spent another moment drying her eyes, then sniffed and turned back to him. Her blue eyes gleamed in the wan light that made it past the shaded windows.

"My husband called me from downtown. He'd been bitten by one of those things, but he'd gotten away from it. They didn't kill him. He was still making his way uptown."

Gartrell didn't really know how to respond to that in any meaningful way. "I'm sorry."

She sniffed again. "So he's one of them now?"

"I don't know. Probably better to keep your mind on your son now."

She looked at him, hard-faced once again. "You *do* know! You've probably got more experience with those things than anyone else in the city!"

Gartrell said nothing, and she turned away from him with a heavy sigh. She rubbed her eyes, then crossed her arms and hugged herself in the gloomy darkness.

"I'm sorry. I don't...I don't mean to fight with you. I'm just wrapped up a little tight right now, you know?"

Gartrell knew all about it, and he felt the same way himself. "It's not a problem. I get where you're coming from. But thinking about your husband right now...well look, there are other things that are more pressing."

Jolie nodded slowly. "Yeah. There are." She turned back to him and tried to relax, but it didn't work. She still looked uptight. The kind of uptight where people start to fray at the edges, and that worried Gartrell a bit. He really didn't need her melting down on him.

Jolie leaned against the stainless steel stove and regarded him for a long moment. "So tell me why you're in New York City. Because I'm thinking you're not really a city boy, are you?"

Gartrell smiled. "Kind of. I'm from a place called Savannah, down in Georgia. Not as big as New York, but not some hick town with a population of six, either."

"I've never been there."

Gartrell shrugged. He figured Jolie wasn't the kind of person to leave NYC for places like Georgia.

"So tell me why you're here," she asked.

Gartrell looked back into the living room. The boy was still fixated on the DVD player, but had taken the straw out of his mouth and had the cup in his lap. Jolie walked toward Gartrell and looked in on her son, then turned back to the first sergeant.

"He'll be occupied for a bit longer."

"Good."

"So tell me what you were doing in New York, Dave."

"Sure."

Gartrell wasn't much of a story teller—his wife said that whenever he had read his once-small children stories, it sounded like he was reading from a chemistry textbook—so he didn't embellish anything, just made a straight, unpretentious report. Working to keep the military acronyms to a minimum, he told Jolie how he was tapped to join Major McDaniels on the mission to New York City, where they linked up with Operational Detachment Alpha 331, call sign OMEN. He had known some of the Special Forces troopers from his time as an instructor, so he had gotten along well with them and had no problem inserting himself into their detachment. He also told her of his history with McDaniels, how he felt the black officer was hidebound by regulation and had only a limited ability to adapt. He had the chops to lead a Special Forces unit; but when it came time to step out of the box, he had problems with his emotions clouding his ability to focus on the mission. When he told her of what had happened in Afghanistan, of how the death of one boy might have saved the lives of five Special Forces soldiers, her eyes widened in surprise.

"You would have killed that boy?"

"If so ordered, yes."

"Was…was that really necessary?"

"He went back and told his people where we were. They came after us with Taliban. Five of our guys went down fighting." Gartrell smiled grimly. "Of course, we sent about two dozen of the stinking Talibs to meet Allah in the process. But that's what we were there for. You understand what I'm saying? McDaniels had the opportunity to balance the scales, and he couldn't do it. No one wanted to kill that boy, not really. Killing kids isn't what we're all about. But letting him go free got a good number of other folks killed. I don't care about the Taliban, they're roaches. But our guys? And the whole village, which the Air Force flattened? That didn't have to happen. The choice was a tough one, but McDaniels called it wrong."

Jolie nodded slowly, thoughtfully. "I see…"

Gartrell went on, relaying how the team had linked up with Wolf Safire and his daughter Regina at Safire's office building.

He had come up with a compound, some sort of vaccine, which would prevent humans from transitioning to the walking dead after they had been bitten. The discovery was obviously quite high-value, so an entire Special Forces Alpha Detachment was dispatched to ensure Safire's safety; McDaniels and Gartrell were Special Operations Command's appointed babysitters to ensure the Safires made it out. And they had almost done just that. They'd actually made it to their helicopters when the stenches overwhelmed the security forces at the assembly area in Central Park. They had even taken off, while the team's second helicopter crashed as the zeds rushed it. The surviving helicopter carrying Gartrell, the Safires, McDaniels, and some other soldiers was on its way out when one of the "window divers"—what Gartrell explained were zeds who literally jumped out of buildings to try and get at food—crashed into their helicopter's main rotor, forcing it to crash land on Lexington Avenue.

So the team took refuge in an office building and waited for aerial extraction from a Marine Corps MV-22 Osprey. But the timing supremely sucked; the building storm that had lashed out at New York City during the night had caused the tiltrotor aircraft to crash as well, leaving the team stranded overnight.

And then, the zeds got inside the building.

Gartrell told her how the Coast Guard had dispatched a cutter to try and evacuate them, and he described in very plain language how the team had fought constantly to cross three city blocks just to get to the East River. It had been the stuff from which nightmares were made; an implacable, seemingly unstoppable enemy numbering in the thousands, intent on running the soldiers and civilians to ground, attacking them again and again. Even as the bodies piled up, the zeds harried them, ignoring their injuries, ignoring the firepower leveled against them, cognizant only of their insatiable hunger. They would go to any length to feed. They were totally, 100% committed in a way that no human being could be. They stripped away the military defenders, a man here, a man there, until finally it was just McDaniels, the civilians, and Gartrell.

And when the final push came, when they had finally made it to the East River, Gartrell diverted the zombies away from the survivors. The mission had to succeed, so that humanity would have a chance against the rising horde. And if that meant First

Sergeant David Gartrell had to sacrifice himself, then so be it. Gartrell didn't paint any flourishes, nor did he tell her just how deeply terrified he had been, striking off on his own, leading the legion of ghouls away from McDaniels and the civilians with a burning flare and not much else. It was just something that had to be done. The mission had to succeed, or else it was lights out for the entire country.

Maybe the entire world.

"And then, I found you at that Starbucks. And here we are, ma'am."

Jolie shook her head slowly. "That…that was some story, Dave."

Gartrell couldn't tell if she was being sarcastic or truthful, so he just nodded. He looked back at Jaden, still staring at the DVD player with rapt attention. His gaze happened upon the dining room table, and the box of shotgun shells sitting there.

"Those shotgun shells. Where's the shotgun that goes with them?"

"I couldn't find it. I found the bullets in one of the open apartments—some young IT guy who thought he was some kind of big game hunter. Disgusting, really." Jolie shook her head in obvious disapproval, and Gartrell didn't volunteer that he was a hunter himself. "Anyway, I meant to go back and look some more, but then it got dark."

"Which apartment?"

She pointed at the ceiling. "On the sixth floor. Apartment A."

"You mind if I go up and take a look around? I might be able to find it. And maybe some other stuff. If this becomes more of an open-ended engagement, we might be here for quite some time, and we'll need to use anything we can find."

Jolie reached for a peach in a nearby bowl and began peeling it with a small paring knife. She worked quickly, expertly, despite the wan light in the galley kitchen. She sliced the peach up and put it in a small plastic bowl.

"His DVD is almost over. Let me give him some food and keep him distracted, and then you can leave. Take one of the backpacks with you. Knock on the door when you come back, and I'll let you in. Just three knocks, okay?"

He nodded. "Three knocks it is." After a moment, he reached out and put a hand on her shoulder. She looked at him, and he smiled as reassuringly as he could.

"I'll be back. I won't be very long."

"I know."

"We're going to get out of this. Believe me, we'll make it."

"Okay."

It was obvious she didn't believe him, but Gartrell didn't waste any time trying to change her mind. He just returned to the bedroom, got the AA-12 and his body armor, helmet, radio, and knapsack. He went back into the dining area and grabbed one of the backpacks. As soon as Jolie began feeding Jaden his peach, Gartrell quietly let himself out of the apartment.

The stairwell was as dark in the day as it had been during the night. Gartrell had brought his night vision goggles with him, so he flipped them down over his eyes and navigated through the all-encompassing darkness as if the stairwell was lit by a sunny day. He went directly to the sixth floor and slowly eased open the stairway door. Switching off the NVGs, he stepped into the hallway beyond, blinking because of the bright light that poured in through the windows at either end. He walked to the apartment marked 6A and tried the door knob; it twisted easily beneath his hand, and he slowly pushed it open with his foot, his AA-12 at the ready.

The apartment beyond had the same layout as Jolie's below, so he was able to conduct his search quickly and efficiently. He kept his distance from the windows, as the drapes were open and he didn't want any of the zeds below to see him. One bedroom had been converted into a sitting room; the other held a master bedroom and the décor indicated it belonged to a bachelor. Gartrell could still smell a faint hint of cologne in the apartment. An expensive multimedia setup was in the living room, dark without power and a little dusty from inexperienced housekeeping. Gartrell went through the bedroom first, casing the closet and attached bathroom. He found nothing terribly useful, so he moved on to the sitting room next door. A large bookcase held many tomes on a wide matter of subjects, from geography to biography. He found a letter opener and tossed it into the backpack—it could serve as a bladed weapon when the time came. He also found several tools: hammers, chisels, screwdrivers, even a small hatchet. He added those to the pack as well. The kitchen yielded nothing, and the vague stink emanating from the closed refrigerator compelled him to ignore it. He searched through the closets and found some rugged outdoors clothes on hangers and a couple of pairs of work boots on the floor. The top shelf had scarves, hats, and a box of old photos. Gartrell ignored all of it and moved on to the small bedroom in the back.

He was startled to find a lion staring at him.

The bedroom had been converted to an office, a true man cave if ever there was one. A lion's head was on one wall. Next to it was an impala's. Facing the lion was a huge water buffalo head, and beside that, a leopard caught in mid-snarl. Gartrell was no stranger to game hunting, but finding these trophies in a small room in New York City was decidedly odd. In the middle of the room sat a desk and a padded chair. Beside the door was a gun cabinet, open and empty. He went through the desk and the built-in bureau, but found nothing other than collectibles from foreign countries, and pictures of a pudgy man in his early thirties posing with various dead beasts: grizzly bears, buffalo, wildebeests, and a huge marlin which must have weighed a thousand pounds.

Guy's gonna need to get himself a bigger room to mount that one.

But still no weapons. Gartrell wouldn't have been surprised if the apartment owner had taken every firearm he had when he left. It would have been the smart thing to do.

Still…

Gartrell returned to the bedroom and shoved the king-sized mattress off the box spring. And there it was—an old but refinished Winchester 42 .410 gauge shotgun, worth probably somewhere in the neighborhood of $4,000. Gartrell picked it up and examined it. The weapon was decades old, definitely a collectible. But to a big game hunter on the run from the zombie horde? Probably not the first weapon of choice, which was why he'd stuffed it under the mattress. No sense leaving it in plain view for it to be stolen by looters, just in case the zeds were defeated before the owner could return to his apartment.

Gartrell took the gun and left it in the hallway.

Apartment 6B was locked. He went up the stairs, ignoring the protesting muscles in his thighs and knees. The apartments on the seventh floor were also locked. As he returned to the stairway, a small, slight sound caught his attention. He stopped at the stairwell door, listening. Was it his imagination?

Then he heard it again. A slight creak from the apartment behind him.

Gartrell's right index finger moved to the AA-12's trigger.

A kind of rolling sound came from behind the door, and Gartrell watched as something passed through the light beneath the door. Something that didn't walk, but seemed to *glide*. Back and forth. Back and forth. And at one point in its transit, a floorboard squeaked. Gartrell moved closer to the door, listening intently. That rolling sound. That squeaking floorboard. As if something on the other side was on wheels…

A wheelchair. The realization hit him suddenly. Of course, a wheelchair. Whomever—or whatever—was in the apartment was confined to a wheelchair, which probably explained why it was still in the building. Waiting for an ambulette or some other service for the disabled to come and evacuate it. A service which never showed up.

So the question is…is it a person, or a zed?

The rolling sound suddenly went from leisurely to outright fast and frantic. Something hit the other side of the metal door with enough force to make the doorbell chime gently, and Gartrell leaped back. The dry moan on the other side of the door told him all he needed to know. There was a zed in the apartment, locked up with no place to go and confined to a wheelchair to boot. It was almost laughable, if not so horrible.

And even worse, the thing on the other side of the door must have been able to sense his presence, or at least had the impression that a hot meal was very close by. It rammed into the door again.

Gartrell dropped back to the stairwell door and opened it as silently as he could. He stepped inside the dark stairwell, flipped down his NVGs, and slowly closed the door behind him. He found a rubber doorstop on the landing, and he shoved it under the door, jamming it in place.

Just in case.

"This is all you got?" Jolie asked when Gartrell returned to the apartment.

"Who lived in apartment seven A?"

"Uh...an old woman. I didn't really know her name, we never saw much of her."

"Was she in a wheelchair?"

"Yes...why?"

"She's still in it."

Jolie looked at him for a long moment. "You mean she wasn't evacuated?"

"Guess not."

"Jesus...she's one of *them*?"

Gartrell nodded. "And locked in her apartment, too. I blocked the stairwell door, but I don't think she's going to be able to get out. So she was either bitten, or she was infected with the virus and died some other way. Jolie, are you *sure* there aren't any zombies in the building?"

"I don't think so. But I haven't been in every apartment." Jolie looked at him directly, brow furrowed. So...what will we do?"

Gartrell shrugged. "Nothing?"

"Nothing? You think it's a good idea to leave one of those *things* in the building with us?" Jolie's voice rose as she spoke, but she caught herself and got under control. She sighed and tried again. "I can't see how leaving one of those things in the building is a good thing."

"I can't kill it without breaking down the door, and that'll make a hell of a lot of noise. Right now, it's contained. We leave it alone until the threat picture changes. It's not going to be able to hurt us for the time being, I guarantee it." Gartrell sighed and looked toward the small bedroom in the back. "But I am wondering if there's any*thing* next door."

"The Skinners are gone. I told you that." Jolie looked down at the stained wood floor.

"Where's Jaden?"

"Taking a nap. He didn't sleep well last night."

Gartrell nodded, and then checked his watch. "Okay, I've got to get in touch with Big Army. I'll do it in the back bedroom. Maybe they'll have an update for us."

That perked her up. "Good."

Gartrell already wore his headset, so he walked into the back bedroom. Jolie followed him and stood in the doorway as he perched himself on the edge of the bed.

"Do you want me to leave you alone?" she asked.

He shook his head. "Not necessary. This isn't going to be a very intimate conversation." He brought the boom microphone closer to his lips and pressed the TRANSMIT button. "Falcon Four, this is Terminator Five, over." He repeated the call three times before he got a response.

"Terminator Five, this is Falcon Four." Falcon sounded a bit rushed. "Listen, we don't have any aviation assets available to us yet. Are you still at the same location? Over."

"Roger Falcon, Terminator's still at the same pos. Street address is one five four zero Second Avenue, apartment four bravo. Fourth floor residence, over."

"Roger that Terminator, good copy. I see it here on the map. Our closest ground units are about thirty blocks north of you, over."

"Roger, Falcon. Any ETA on the aviation units? Over."

"Terminator, this is Falcon. Units are en route from Pennsylvania, and it's about a hundred and fifty mile trip, so they won't arrive for another hour. After that, refuel, preflight, and then whatever's on the air tasking order. You're on the list, but I don't know where you fall in order of importance, sorry. Over."

"Roger, Falcon. It would be advisable to try and extract us during daylight if possible. Like I said, I have a special needs child with me, and he's going to get super-stressed with things in daylight, much less at night. Over."

"Terminator, Falcon—roger all."

"Falcon, this is Terminator. Can you give me a rundown on current events, please? What's the troop disposition? Over."

"Very quickly, Terminator. We have units who made it into the subway system, as you recommended. Radio contact with them is extremely sporadic, and it seems they can only make contact when they're at a station...I guess because that's where the ground is broken by the entrances to the stations or something like that. Contact with zed has been minimal, and so far, ninety-five percent of all the engagements have gone our way. Zed is definitely in the subway system, but not in great numbers, and like you said they're not that great at nocturnal operations. Over."

"Falcon, Terminator. Glad to be of help. What else do you have for me? Over."

"Terminator, Falcon…not much else right now. We'll talk again in sixty minutes, over."

Gartrell sighed. "Roger, Falcon. I'll be back with you in sixty minutes. Terminator, out."

"What did they say?" Jolie asked.

Gartrell pulled his headset off his ears and let it hang around the back of his neck. He reached for one of the plastic bottles of water on the small bureau and took a long pull from it before answering.

"Helicopters haven't arrived yet. Some light infantry units are pushing into the city through the subway tunnels, but there's no way they can move any heavy equipment through the streets—everything's blocked, by abandoned vehicles if not the stenches themselves."

"The ones coming through the subway tunnels…will they—"

"I get the idea they're on zed hunts. The Army probably wants to close down the tunnels as an escape point for the zombies. I doubt they'll come up to the surface streets. And if they do, they won't be doing it for us, it'll be because they got chased out of the tunnels by a couple of thousand zeds. And then they'll be in pretty much the same position we are." Gartrell drank more water, then looked over his shoulder at the closet at the foot of the bed. He scooted over and pulled it open. A few boxes were inside, stacked against the wall. Gartrell pulled them out and tossed them on the bed, then knocked on the wall.

"So you're sure the apartment next door is empty?" he asked.

"Yeah. The Skinners, they're gone, like I said."

"Fantastic." Gartrell rose and pushed past her. He walked into the living room and picked up the backpack with the tools inside, then headed back to the bedroom. Jolie followed him, a puzzled expression on her face.

"What are you going to do, Dave?"

Gartrell dumped the tools on the bed and picked out a small sledgehammer and several chisels. He then emptied the closet completely, tossing old men's clothes on the floor.

"I'm going to make us a place to fall back to in case the shit hits the fan." He knocked on the wall several times, in different places. It felt solid to him, and he imagined he was faced with plaster over brick, or maybe cinderblock. That didn't make things any easier, but he hadn't expected it to be sheetrock. He picked up the sledgehammer and tapped it against the wall, and plaster fractured and fell away. Sure enough, there was red brick behind it. He looked over at Jolie.

"You're going to knock a hole through the wall?"

"Like I said, we might need a place to fall back to. It won't be much, but it'll buy us some time. I'll try to be as quiet as I can, but you might want to close the door behind you. Try and make sure Jaden doesn't get too upset if he wakes up. All right?"

"All right." She stepped out of the small bedroom and slowly closed the door behind her.

It took well over two hours since he had to keep the noise to a minimum, but Gartrell finally cut through the back of the closet and into the apartment next door. Jolie checked on him from time to time, and even Jaden showed up, watching Gartrell hack away at the wall with hammers and chisels. The plaster was gone within minutes; it took almost two hours to chisel through the mortar holding the bricks together, and then he had to pull those out one by one. He took a break to call Falcon on the hour, but there was still no news. Gartrell figured the public affairs officer on the other end of the radio really wasn't plugged in to anything much at all, but there was nothing he could do about that other than continually plead his case and beg for information.

Of course, the only thing that mattered were the helicopters, and they either hadn't arrived or the 10th Mountain Division had more pressing priorities for them to attend to.

Finally, Gartrell punched through the plaster on the other side of the wall, and he peered through the small hole he had made. Half the view was blocked by a table leg, but room beyond was sunlit. He surmised the apartment on the other side of the wall was a mirror image of Jolie's, and that he had cut through to another small bedroom. He pulled more bricks away, sneezing from the dust, until the hole was big enough for him to squeeze through. Jaden was delighted by the sudden change in the back bedroom, and he pranced about on his toes, hooting a bit. Gartrell shushed him, but he still had to smile. There was something so innocent about the boy's delight that Gartrell couldn't help himself. Jolie picked Jaden up and hugged him tight as Gartrell unholstered his sidearm and pushed himself through the hole in the closet wall.

The apartment was empty, as Jolie had said it would be. Gartrell walked through it and checked every room. He found evidence the occupants had left in a hurry—a carton of milk sat spoiling on the counter, magazines and books had been knocked from some shelves, and clothes lay scattered about on the floor in front of the closets. There was no luggage to speak of; the family had obviously taken that with them. He found a bowl of Hershey's Kisses and unwrapped one of the chocolates and popped it into his mouth, then placed the bowl on top of the refrigerator so Jaden wouldn't find it. The last thing he needed was a four-year-old autistic boy hopped up on sugar.

"Dave? Jaden wants to come through," Jolie called through the hole in the wall.

"Put his shoes on first. And wait for me to close the curtains, some of them are still open." Gartrell sidled up to a window and peeked out, keeping as close to the wall as possible. They were still out there, the legions of the dead...but something was different. They were no longer just milling about, shambling aimlessly to and fro. Somehow, some way, they had oriented themselves toward the north. As Gartrell watched, the ghoulish monstrosities lurched and stumbled up Second Avenue.

In the far, far distance, he thought he heard the crackle of small arms fire.

They're on the hunt for food. They know there are people up north, so they're moving out, looking to get the a la carte special.

He watched the bizarre migration for a moment, and started counting stenches. He stopped at a hundred and three, which he had counted in less than forty seconds. There were hundreds right outside the apartment building, and thousands more walking up the avenue behind them.

Unreal.

Gartrell closed the curtains in the apartment as inconspicuously as he could. A scuffling sound attracted his attention, and he hurried back to the small bedroom just as Jaden walked through the hole in the wall. He looked at Gartrell and smiled, his previous aloofness forgotten. He kicked a brick across the wood floor and giggled.

"Easy now," Gartrell said. "Not too much noise, okay?"

Jaden babbled something and walked on his toes toward the bedroom door, flapping his hands in the air. Gartrell reached out and restrained him gently. Jaden pushed against his hand, not because he didn't want to be touched, but because the adventure of exploring a new and different apartment beckoned to him like a siren's song. Gartrell looked back at the hole in the wall and watched as Jolie pushed herself through. She stood up straight and brushed dust from her shoulders.

"Nice job," she said to Gartrell.

"Thanks. But I usually do my best work with explosives."

Jolie smiled and took Jaden's hand. He pulled her along behind him as he surged out of the small bedroom and into the Skinners' apartment. Gartrell hung back for a moment, and pulled on his radio headset.

"Falcon Four, this is Terminator Five, over." He waited. "Falcon Four, Terminator Five with a SITREP for you, over." SITREP was military shorthand for situation report, the circumstances where one unit or individual passed on tactical information. He didn't know if what he had witnessed outside was a localized phenomenon, but he felt the lightfighters should know about it. He repeated the call twice more and was about to give up when Falcon came on the line.

"Terminator, this is Falcon...what've you got? Over."

"Falcon, Terminator. Don't know how it happened, but these things look kind of organized now. They're all moving in the same direction at the same time, heading northerly at a slow but steady pace." As he spoke, Gartrell moved to the skinny window in the bedroom and peeked around the curtain. Sure enough, the great stench migration continued, with all corpses ambulating north up Second Avenue. Gartrell noticed for the first time that there was a subway station right across the street, on the far corner. He remembered that another one was on his side of the avenue, just outside the Starbucks.

"I thought you guys would want to know that, Falcon. Over."

"Roger, Terminator. We're getting some aerial surveillance pictures from our UAVs. It's not just your neighborhood, it's everywhere in the city. The zeds are picking up and marching north. Over."

"It's the zombie chow line, Falcon. Get ready for it. Over."

"Roger that, Terminator. By the way, news for you. First Chinook unit is setting down right now. We're using the parking lots outside of Yankee Stadium as an assembly area. We already have HEMT-T tankers there," Falcon reported. He pronounced HEMT-T as "hemmit", and Gartrell knew they were huge, multi-wheeled trucks that could be configured for a variety of missions, in this case transporting aviation fuel. "Summit Six is lobbying to get a bird out to you directly. He wants you here, as a source of intel. Over."

"Falcon, this is Terminator. Tell Six I'll even fetch his coffee and give him foot rubs if he can get us out of here—though do pass on that I'm hardly an expert at either. Over."

Falcon laughed over the radio. "Good one, Terminator. I'll pass that on. If you—"

Jolie shrieked suddenly from somewhere in the apartment, and Gartrell tuned out Falcon as he bolted out of the bedroom, his pistol ready in his right hand. He found Jolie kneeling on the floor, clutching Jaden to her as Jaden reached past her shoulder for the curtains. Gartrell saw he'd already been able to pull them half-open.

"Is everything all right? What happened?" he asked, hurrying toward them.

"Dah. Dee," Jaden said gently, still reaching for the window.

"He's out there," Jolie said. Her voice quaked in fear, and her shoulders shook. "Jaden opened the curtains before I could stop him…and when I looked out, *I saw him outside*."

"You saw *who* outside?"

She looked up at him, and tears spilled from her big blue eyes. "Jack. My husband. Jared's father."

"Dah. Dee."

"Terminator, this is Falcon…you still there? Over."

"Falcon, Terminator. Stand by, something's up on my end, over." Gartrell stepped past them and peeked past the open curtain at the street below. The stenches were still walking north, but there was a congregation of about ten or fifteen standing right below. One of them—a man in a blood-spattered French blue shirt blazer and tan slacks—looked up at the apartment building with flat, dead eyes, his face pale and bloodless. A huge rent had been torn through his bearded cheek, and one of his hands was wrapped up in a bloodstained handkerchief. Flies flitted about the corpses below. Gartrell watched as they crawled in and out of the man-thing's mouth and nostrils. The stench didn't appear to care; it just stared up at the building.

At the windows of the apartment next door. Jolie and Jaden's apartment.

"Dah. Dee," Jaden said again, and this time there was an edge to his voice.

"Take him out of here," Gartrell said. He moved the pistol's fire selector to SAFE and slid it into its holster, his eyes still on the group of zeds below. As he watched, the stench he figured to be Jolie's husband—who in the pictures on the wall was hale and hearty, unlike this scraggly figure below—reached into one of its trouser pockets. It pulled something out and, for the first time, slowly looked down. It opened its hand and stared at what lay inside.

It was a key ring.

Oh, fuck me. Gartrell thought he had seen it all when zeds drove vehicles and fired guns, but if they could start unlocking doors with keys…that was even worse, somehow.

"Dah-dee!" Jaden said, this time with much more force.

"Take him back to your apartment!" Gartrell shook Jolie's shoulder. "Jolie! Get him out of here! *Now!*"

"All right!" she snapped back, her voice marred by a sudden sob. "We're going!" She picked up Jaden and hurried back to the bedroom, sniffling. Jaden struggled against her, but she held him tight. Gartrell turned back to the window and slowly edged closer. Sure enough, Jolie's dead husband was going through the keys on the ring, and he finally settled on one. Moving with a stupid slowness, the ghoul advanced toward the apartment building, holding the key out before it like it was some sort of weapon. Gartrell leaned forward a bit more to keep eyeballs on target, but he saw other zeds look up in his direction. He stepped back from the window and headed for the apartment door. He unlocked it and double-checked to ensure that he could open the door from the hall and that he wouldn't get locked out. He ran toward the stairway across from Jolie's apartment, and as he reached for the door, he realized he wasn't wearing his helmet—and his NVGs were still mounted on the helmet's bracket. He dithered about for an instant, wondering if he should go back for it, then decided he didn't have the time. He pushed open the stairwell door and kept it open with one foot as he looked down over the banister.

Below, the darkness was total, complete, unbroken. Gartrell heard the sound of his own breathing, loud in his ears, magnified by the tight confines of the stairwell. He put a hand on the butt of his pistol, and waited.

From below, he heard something, a distant banging noise. He recalled the glass in the apartment building's front door was reinforced with wire, and thought that one or two zombies would be unable to break through it. But what about five? Or ten?

The banging stopped, but other sounds slowly rose up the stairwell. The crash of a door flung against a wall. A distant moaning. A far-off shuffling of feet...

Fuck, they're inside!

As if to bring the point home, light flooded into the bottom of the stairwell as the door on the first floor was pushed open. Shadows filled the light, shadows in the shape of human beings.

Gartrell had seen enough. He pulled back and closed the door to the stairs behind him and hurried for the apartment at the end of the hall.

"Falcon, this is Terminator, over."

"Terminator, this is Falcon. What's happening down there? Over."

"Falcon, Terminator." Gartrell stepped inside the Skinners' apartment and locked the door behind him. "I'm suffering from some major déjà vu, this is the second time in less than twenty-four hours the building I'm in is overrun by stenches, and it's not getting any easier with practice. I've got maybe a dozen stenches on their way up, over." As he spoke, Gartrell sprinted for the hole he had cut in the closet wall and pushed through it. He went straight to the bureau and donned his helmet and body armor, then collected the remains of his gear. He put water bottles in his pockets and ensured the grenades were close at hand. He would need them soon.

"Jolie! Load up one of those backpacks with as much food and water as you can carry, and get your revolver and that shotgun. We're leaving!"

She appeared at the door, still holding Jaden. "Where will we go?"

Gartrell pointed at the hole in the wall. She started to say something else, but he waved her to silence.

"Ma'am, listen to me. The stenches are on their way up. You want to save that little boy of yours? Do as I tell, and do it damned quick." Falcon was speaking into his ears, and he put a hand to one of the ear phones. "Falcon, Terminator. Say again, over."

"Terminator, this is Falcon. They're hot-refueling one of the Chinooks. They'll come for you as soon as they can. Twenty minutes, tops. Over."

"Not sure we can hold out for ten minutes, Falcon. I've got a little over a hundred rounds of ammunition total, not really enough to hold down the fort." He slipped on his knapsack and pulled out the remaining drum of 12-gauge ammunition for the AA-12. He swapped out the almost-depleted one—down to three shells!—and slapped on the new one. "Falcon, how many soldiers are in the Second Avenue subway line? Over."

"Terminator, Falcon…uh, not really sure at the moment, why do you ask? Over."

"Because there's a station right in front of the apartment building, and it might be our only chance. If we can stay ahead of the zeds and link up with the lightfighters, we might have a good chance of getting out of here. I'd love to catch a ride on that Chinook, but twenty minutes is a long wait under our circumstances, and if something goes wrong and the chopper has to abort, we'll be trapped on the roof and royally fucked. So I really need to know if there are any troops in the area, how many, and if they're headed our way. And I need to know that real, real quick. Over."

"Roger that, Terminator. Stand by."

Gartrell checked all of his weapons. All were operational. He strapped the MP5 to his right thigh and pulled the carry rig's Velcro straps tight. He ensured elbow and kneepads were in place, and slipped on his gloves. He then dropped the baby sledge and two big chisels into his knapsack; he couldn't imagine them coming in handy in the short term, but he wouldn't want to wind up needing them and regret not having them. Everything in order, he left the bedroom and walked to the living room, where Jolie frantically stuffed one of the backpacks with virtually everything on the table. Gartrell grabbed her arm, and she swatted him away.

"I've got this!" she said, and the angry tone in her voice set off Jaden. He started wailing and jumping around the room, flapping his hands. Gartrell could smell his full diaper, and he reached out and grabbed Jaden with one hand, pulling him toward Jolie.

"I'll take care of it," Gartrell said calmly. "Jaden needs you right now. Let's get him changed, give him some water, and then move to the next apartment. We have a little bit of time, but the zeds are on their way up. They're in the stairwell. Do you understand what I'm saying? We're about to get very danger close."

Jolie looked at him with wide eyes. "They're…coming? Is my husband…?"

Gartrell nodded, and Jolie put a hand to her mouth and looked away. Gartrell grabbed her chin and forced her to look at him.

"I don't want Jaden to see that thing," he said, "and neither do you. So let's get a move on. We're running out of time."

Jolie nodded and grabbed Jaden. She cooed in his ear, trying to get him to calm down. Gartrell dumped out the contents of the backpack and started over. Water. Some food. Some juice. Diapers for Jaden. Wet wipes. A small blanket. He then hurried into Jaden's room while Jolie changed the boy's diaper. She looked at him but didn't ask what he was doing. Inside the bright, cheerily painted room, Gartrell opened the closet and went through the clothes there. He pulled out several pairs of jeans, three long-sleeved shirts, a few undershirts, and several pairs of socks. He found a pair of toddler shoes with an aggressive tread on them, and carried everything outside. He put the garments inside a plastic bag and put the bag inside the backpack. The shoes went in an outside pocket that he zipped up tight. In another pocket he put in the LED lights and a flashlight and spare batteries.

"Terminator, Falcon. Come in, Terminator."

"Falcon, Terminator. Give me the good news, over."

"Terminator, we have one light infantry platoon that's a company advance element about ten blocks north of your position, in the T-line tunnels. We haven't been able to contact them yet, but they are due to report in soon. There's another unit in the Q line, and we just notified them of your situation—they'll try and raise the platoon in the Second Avenue tunnel. They might have better luck than we will in the short term. Chinook is still refueling, and I've been told the aviators are going to head your way, over."

"Roger that, Falcon. Is that all you've got?" The news left Gartrell feeling spectacularly underwhelmed, but there wasn't much sense in berating the man on the other end of the radio link. Even though a full division was supposedly camped out across the river from Manhattan, getting it into the city was a major operation itself, and it would take several more hours to secure the zone.

"Terminator, we're working to chop some Apaches your direction for close air, but that's all I've got right now. We're working on it. Over."

Gartrell zipped up the backpack and looked at Jolie. She had Jaden calmed down a bit now, and he was drinking water from a Sippy cup. The boy was still quite disorganized, and he looked remote and detached from the current events. He stared up at the ceiling as his mother zipped up his jeans. Gartrell watched them both for a long moment, and he wondered how he could possibly save both of them.

Seize the initiative, dumbass.

"Jolie, I'm going to have to make a whole lot of racket. Cover Jaden's ears. I'll need to open the window in the back bedroom."

"What are you going to do?"

"I'm going to give us some cover."

Jolie pulled Jaden into her arms and didn't say anything further. Gartrell grabbed the backpack and carried it into the bedroom and shoved it through the hole into the next apartment. He then tore away the tape holding the window in place and opened the window. The air outside was only mildly warm, and the sun had set behind the buildings across the street. The avenue below was in light shadow. There were hundreds of zombies in the street. Most were still headed north, but several made their way toward the apartment building. Directly below, there was a large cluster of zeds pushing and shoving each other as they tried to get into the building. Many more than he could possibly kill with the amount of ammunition he had on hand.

Oh fuck.

He pulled his pistol and stuck it out the window. He aimed at a big Cadillac down below and fired three shots into its trunk. The pistol reports were loud and sharp, and they echoed throughout the concrete canyon of Second Avenue. Hundreds of stenches looked up and moaned when they saw Gartrell, and a new rush of decrepit corpses surged toward the apartment building's entrance. Gartrell ignored the ruckus and leaned out the narrow window and stared at the Cadillac. He saw a wet stream slowly emerge from behind the vehicle. Zombies stepped through the trickle of gasoline without noticing it; their attention remained riveted on what they hoped was their next meal.

Overhead, glass shattered. Gartrell sensed movement, and he ducked back into the bedroom as shards of glass fell to the street, raining down on the ghouls below. And then a slight, wasted corpse streaked past the window, bouncing off the apartment building's façade as it went, its white, dirty hair trailing behind it. The zombie screeched as it reached for him with hands twisted from a long battle with arthritis, but it didn't even touch the window sill. Gartrell leaned forward and watched the corpse slam into the sidewalk with enough force to shatter its arms and, he suspected, its spine. But the body of the old woman from the seventh floor still moved. Twitching and hitching, it turned toward the apartment building's entrance, trailing its useless legs behind it as it crawled. The rest of the zombie horde fairly trampled the new arrival, unaware of its presence beneath their feet.

Gartrell pulled the last fragmentation grenade he had from the clip on his body armor. He kissed the cold metal orb, yanked the pin free, and lobbed it toward the Cadillac. The safety spoon flew off with a metallic *ping!* that he could still hear over the undulating mass of moaning carcasses below. The grenade struck a zed right in the skull and left a good-sized dent in it before it hit the street and rolled toward the car. It disappeared beneath the shiny black Caddy.

All hell broke loose.

The explosion was strong enough to rattle windows in every building overlooking the street. The Cadillac fairly leaped into the air as the grenade's explosion momentarily superheated the air beneath it and ignited the fumes emanating from its punctured fuel tank. A column of bright fire chased away the shadows in the street, and Gartrell slammed the window closed as the mushroom cloud of flame and smoke rushed into the sky.

"Dave! Dave, what's going on?" Jolie shouted from the living room. There was pure panic in her voice, and Jaden was shrieking.

Gartrell hurried through the kitchen and into the living room. Jolie and Jaden were huddled together on the living room floor. He knelt beside them and touched Jaden's head gently. He continued crying anyway.

"We're probably going to have to leave this building and head for the subway," he told Jolie. "There are other soldiers in the tunnels who can link up with us and lead us to safety. But in order for us to have even a fifty-fifty chance of making it to the subway station alive, I had to give us some cover." Another blast shook the building again as a second car exploded into flames. "The second stairway, across the hall from the next apartment— where would it take us?"

"To an exit on Eighty-Sixth Street," she said. "But Dave, I thought they would send a helicopter—"

"It'll never get here in time. Get Jaden pulled together as well as you can." He got to his feet and picked up the shotgun. He cycled it, testing its action—everything worked perfectly. He opened the box of .410 shells. They looked old, but Gartrell was confident they would still fire. He loaded one into the old shotgun and pumped it, dropping the shell into the chamber. He loaded another five into the weapon until it was full, then returned to the bedroom and placed the small-bore weapon in the next apartment. As he returned to Jolie's apartment, he saw Jaden run into the entry foyer. Jolie ran after him, her eyes wide.

"*Jaden,*" she said, but her voice was nothing more than a strangled whisper.

Gartrell spun around and looked on as she caught up to Jaden and grabbed him. She pulled him away from the door, hugging him to her chest. He resisted quietly, and reached toward the door.

Gartrell almost jumped as one of the deadbolts unlocked with a startlingly loud click.

Oh please, kid…don't say a word…

"Dah-dee," Jaden said.

Whatever was on the other side of the door heard the small voice, and it grunted and slammed against the door with all its might. More ghouls in the hallway outside the apartment moaned, and the door shook and trembled as they added their bodies to the fray. Gartrell heard metal scraping against metal, and he knew the former man of the house was about to unlock the remaining deadbolt, which would leave only the security chain as their last defense.

Gartrell ran back to the kitchen. He grabbed the refrigerator and pulled it toward him. It rolled easily on casters, so he quickly pulled it out of its recess. He yanked the power cord out of the wall socket and pushed the bulky, stainless steel appliance into the entry foyer.

"Get out of the way!" he snapped to Jolie as she dragged Jaden away from the door. Once they were clear, Gartrell upended the refrigerator. Ceramic chips flew through the air and ricocheted off the walls as it slammed to the floor and shattered several expensive floor tiles in the process. Gartrell wasted no time and rammed the appliance against the apartment's entry door just as the last deadbolt flipped open and the door started to open. Gartrell slammed it shut with the refrigerator. He angled the huge appliance and wedged it in place in the narrow entry hall. It wouldn't hold forever, but it would give them enough time to retreat.

Gartrell ran to Jolie and Jaden. Jaden had retreated inside himself again, and he stared at the ceiling with blank, vacant eyes. Jolie hugged him to her tightly, half-crouching in the living room, staring at the apartment door as it opened an inch and slammed into the refrigerator. Her face was frozen in a rictus of terror. Gartrell reached out and cupped her chin in his hand and forced her to look at him.

"Jolie…stay with me, God damn it!" He was done treating her as a helpless civilian; the only way to get through to her was to treat her like a soldier.

"Yes," she said, her voice small. "I'm here."

"Then listen to me. Do everything I say. Don't think about it, just *do* it. If you stop to think, they'll get you. If you act when I tell you to, you and your boy will get out of this alive. I guarantee it." Her eyes turned back to the door, and he shook her roughly. "Are you *with* me, Jolie?"

She looked back at him, and the fear in her big blue eyes receded a fraction. "Yes. I'm with you," she said, and her voice was stronger this time.

"Do you have your gun?"

"Yes."

"Was all the ammunition for it on the table?"

"Yes."

Gartrell nodded. That meant he'd put all of it in the backpack. "Take Jaden to the next apartment. Put on the backpack, and get the shotgun. Take Jaden into the kitchen there and wait for me." The door banged into the refrigerator again and again, and the racket was getting louder. Gartrell heard metal slide across shattered ceramic, and he turned. The door was open several inches now, and as he watched, arms reached in and flailed about crazily, searching for something to grab. Something warm.

"Time's up. Remember, do as I tell you, and don't stop to think about it—just do it. Do it for Jaden."

"All right."

"Then get going!"

Jolie carried Jaden into the rear bedroom, moving as fast as she could. Gartrell ran to the bookcase and dumped all the books onto the floor. He reached into his pocket and pulled out a book of matches emblazoned with a small pig next to the legend *The Barbeque Hut* on the cover. He struck a match and held it to one of the paperbacks. Once it caught, he struck a second match and lit another book on fire, then another, and another. Once the blaze started going strong, he tossed cushions from the couch onto it. Foul, black smoke rose into the air. The zeds in the hallway crashed against the door, and the refrigerator slid another few inches. Gartrell retreated to the back bedroom, pulled the pocket door shut, and shoved the bed against it. He darted into the bathroom and pulled the box of cotton balls off the medicine cabinet shelf, then bolted into the closet. He closed its cheap, flimsy door behind him and crawled through the hole into the next apartment.

He looked up to find Jolie had him covered with the shotgun. Jaden lay on the floor beside her, sobbing softly. Gartrell nodded to Jolie approvingly.

"Exactly what I want to see," he said. "Be aggressive, and always be ready to shoot. That's what your life is right now, you understand?"

"That should be obvious," she said. She'd pulled herself together, and she'd donned the backpack like he'd told her. She slowly lowered the weapon.

Gartrell pointed at the shotgun. "You have six rounds in that, and it's loaded with birdshot. You need to fire at their heads when they get close. Don't shoot at anything more than twenty feet away, the shot isn't big enough to do enough damage. Inside of twenty feet, fire right at their kissers. Get it?"

"Got it. Do I smell smoke?"

"Yes you do. We're not going to be able to stay here, so I'm making it a little tougher for them to track us. Where's your revolver?"

She lifted her jacket and he saw the butt of the .38 sticking out of the waistband of her jeans. Gartrell would have preferred she kept it in a holster, but he'd forgotten to ask if she had one. He told her to try to carry it in her jacket pocket. She did as he suggested, and it fit fine. He then walked behind her and pulled the pistol ammo from the backpack and put it in her other pocket. He loaded up the jacket's breast pockets with shotgun shells, and ejected one shell from the shotgun and described how to load it. He then handed her the expelled shell and watched her load it into the shotgun.

"Okay, we're going to get out of here now. We're going to leave this apartment and go straight across the hall to the stairway. We're going down until we hit the exit, then we're going directly to the subway station. When we get there, I want you to grab onto my belt and hold on, because it's going to be pitch black and I'm the only one who can see." He touched his night vision goggles to make his point.

"How will we get there?"

He patted the AA-12 hanging at his side. "By fighting our way through."

She swallowed. "But what about Jaden?"

Gartrell reached into one of his pockets and pulled out several white plastic quick ties. "We'll have to tie him to my back, and we'll have to go like bats out of hell. Not my first choice, but we're pressed for time."

"You intend to tie up my son?"

"Like I said, not my first choice. But this is where we are. Unless you have any other ideas? I don't think we want to take a chance with him running off, or slowing us down. Right?"

"I…I don't have any other ideas, but…"

Gartrell handed her the box of cotton balls. "Stuff your ears with those, then help me with Jaden. Once he's on my back, put cotton in his ears too. Things are going to get loud."

Her expression quiet and resigned, she did as he asked. Gartrell turned away from her and knelt beside Jaden. He gently touched the boy, and Jaden looked at him. Gartrell felt a twinge of guilt; the kid looked miserable, and beneath the heavy veil of his autism, there was no way to make him understand what was happening. He was 100% Victim to everything that was going on.

"Hang in there, Jaden," he said softly, brushing the boy's red hair away from his face. "Be strong for your momma, okay?"

"Momma," he said, and sobbed some more.

"Momma's right here," Jolie said. She knelt beside him, and he reached for her. Jolie took him into her arms and hugged him tightly, her eyes closed. Tears ran past her eyelids, leaving glistening trails on her cheeks. Gartrell realized she was basically hugging her child goodbye. He wanted to say something to her, something encouraging, something motivating…but there just wasn't anything to be said. Jolie had never been schooled in the art of warfare, but she wasn't stupid. She knew their chances were pretty piss-poor, no matter what Gartrell might have said.

Gartrell got to his feet and stepped away from them, giving the mother and her child a last few moments of privacy. He slipped the quick ties back inside his pocket, then depressed the push-to-talk button on his radio. "Falcon, this is Terminator Five, over."

"Terminator, this is Falcon. Go ahead, over."

"Falcon, Terminator's danger close and we have to leave the building. Unless you have some great news and can tell me that Chinook is on its way. Over."

"Ah, Terminator, Falcon. Negative, Chinook is still refueling. The aviators won't leave without full tanks, they don't want to leave anything to chance while over zed country, over."

"Roger that, Falcon. We're going for the subway station. I've got NVGs, so it'll at least even the odds a bit. You've got troops in the T line tunnels? Over."

"Terminator, Falcon. Roger, we have an entire company moving down the line, clearing it out. Like I told you, one platoon is moving ahead of the rest of the company, over."

"Falcon, give me that frequency for that platoon, over."

"Terminator, Falcon. Stand by." As Gartrell waited, he could smell the smoke from the apartment next door. He walked toward the hole in the wall and knelt before it. He definitely heard something going on over there as well—the zeds were breaking down the door and forcing their way inside. He hoped the cushions emitted enough smoke to keep them dumb and blind for a little while longer. "Terminator, Falcon's back with you. Frequency is one two seven point eight gigahertz, and Delta Company's call sign is Destroyer. The detached platoon is Pathfinder One. Over."

"Roger that, Falcon. I can make that frequency. Have you been in contact with Pathfinder? Over."

"Negative on that last, Terminator. Waiting for them to report in, and will advise them as soon as they do of your plan, over."

"Roger that, Falcon." Gartrell heard something slam against the bedroom door in Jolie's apartment. He dragged a heavy coffee table over and upended it against the hole in the wall, then shoved a chair against it, dragging it around Jolie and Jaden as they clung to each other. It wasn't much of a barricade, but it would serve to delay the stenches for a minute or two. "Terminator's got to pull out now, Falcon. I'm rolling over to the company frequency of one two seven point eight, would be appreciative if you could switch over with me and give me a radio check, over."

"Roger, Terminator. Switching over now."

Gartrell switched his radio over to the new frequency and transmitted his identity. Falcon wasn't there, but he did get Summit Six.

"Good to hear from you again, Terminator. Falcon told me what you're up to, heading out into the streets and all," the infantry commander said. "You've got big brass ones, Green Beret. Over."

"Always have, always will, Six. Give Falcon my regards, and he gets some beers from me once this is over. Do me a favor, Six, and make sure your lightfighters get the word we're coming down. Unit of three, myself, one female, one four-year-old boy with autism. If we get boxed in, we're going to need every swinging dick we can get. Over."

"Roger that, Terminator. We're headed your way. Good luck, first sergeant—we'll be listening in on this side. Summit Six, out here."

More noise from the other side of the wall, and Gartrell thought he heard the sound of the bed being pushed against the wall. He darted toward the apartment door and looked through the security peephole. There was some smoke in the hallway, but not enough to substantially reduce visibility. Gartrell pulled his last smoke grenade from his belt and unlocked the door as quietly as he could. With a silent prayer, he slowly pulled the door open and peeked around the sill.

There were zeds, at least a dozen of them, all fighting to get into Jolie's apartment. All were fixated on that particular task, snarling and moaning as they jostled against each other, oblivious to anything else. Gartrell pulled the pin from the smoker and rolled it down the hallway and closed the door as it went off and commenced spewing gray-white smoke. He didn't bother to lock the door, just left it closed.

He ran back into the living room and knelt beside Jolie and Jaden. He pulled the quick ties from his pocket once again and touched Jolie on the shoulder.

"It's time. Let's get Jaden secured, and then we're on our way."

Jolie hugged her boy one final time, then looked at Gartrell. "He'll probably scream. You know that."

Gartrell nodded. "We just have to get him restrained as quickly as possible, at least until we get into the subway tunnel. I'll clear a path through the zeds, you just keep up and make sure they don't flank me, all right?"

"I'll try."

"Well, try real, real hard—your son's going to be on *my* back, remember. Now let's cut some butt, we're out of time."

Jaden struggled but didn't scream as much as Gartrell feared he would. It still took almost two minutes to get the boy secured to Gartrell's back, and Jolie fought back more tears as she bound her son's wrists and ankles so tightly they must have hurt. Jaden jerked and pulled, repeating "No, no, no!" again and again, but at last, he was strapped in place against the back of Gartrell's body armor.

There was a crash from Jolie's apartment as the stenches flooded into the bedroom. A moment later, they found their way into the closet, and the coffee table rocked back and forth as a zed pushed against it. Gartrell grabbed Jolie's hand and pulled her with him as he made a beeline for the door, his battered combat boots whispering across expensive Persian rugs.

"You open the door, and I'll clear whatever's on the other side. You'll go past me and open the door to the stairwell across the hall. Wait for me there. Once we're in, grab Jaden's shoulder and follow me down the stairs. Did you put cotton in his ears?"

"Yes."

"Good. It's going to be very smoky outside in the hall, but we won't be in it for long. Let's go." He raised the AA-12 to his shoulder, barrel pointed at the floor and nodded toward the door. Jolie grabbed the door knob in her right hand and looked back at him. Gartrell nodded again, and she yanked the door open.

A mass of unpleasant-smelling gray-white smoke billowed in. Gartrell stepped into the hallway as Jaden moaned and struggled, uncomfortable with the sudden action and the stress it put on his wrists and ankles. A zombie moved against the wall nearby, feeling its way along with outstretched arms. It was vague and indistinct in the dense smoke, and it did not seem to notice Gartrell even though he stood no more than ten feet away. He saw why that was—both its eyes were gone, leaving only empty sockets in the flesh-covered skull. Gartrell kept it covered anyway as Jolie moved past him without hesitation. He caught the apartment door before it slammed shut and closed it gently, then faded into the smoke as the zombie crept slowly closer. It emitted a long, drawn out moan. It couldn't see them, but sensed the presence of the living somewhere in the hallway. Gartrell moved to the right, edging toward the stairwell door which Jolie held open. He stepped onto the dark landing, and Jolie closed the door behind him. The darkness inside was complete, and Jaden made a small mewling sound in the back of his throat. Gartrell flipped down his night vision goggles and took them out of standby mode, and the stairwell was clearly revealed to him in shades of green and white. He turned and grabbed Jolie's hand and put it on his shoulder. She clutched him, strong enough to hurt, and Jaden mewled again, his voice echoing in the concrete-walled stairwell. Gartrell started down, walking slowly enough that Jolie could find her footing. It took her a moment to synchronize her movements with his, but she learned quickly, and soon they were making good progress. As they descended, Gartrell heard voices over the radio: the light infantry platoon reporting their progress, and Summit Six ordering them to advance with all possible haste to link up with Gartrell and the civilians. Gartrell felt a blossom of hope spread open in his chest.

"Terminator Five, this is Summit Six. Are you still on this frequency, over?"

Gartrell keyed his transmit button twice. He didn't want to talk in the stairwell; even a whisper would carry farther than he wanted it to.

"Terminator Five, Summit Six. Understand you cannot talk, over."

Gartrell clicked the transmit button twice once again.

"Terminator Five, Summit Six. Pathfinder is aware of your circumstances, and they are proceeding to the Eighty-Sixth Street station. Double-click if you get that, over."

Gartrell did as instructed.

"Terminator, Summit. You should be hearing helicopters soon. These are not the transports, I say again, these are not transports—they are Apaches from the Tenth Mountain aviation brigade, and they are to give you fire support. As soon as you're ready to make your run for the subway, let me know and we'll get them lined up for close-in gunnery, over."

Gartrell's spirits fairly soared. He double-clicked the transmit button again, and he started walking faster, pulling Jolie along. She stumbled on one step, and he forced himself to slow down as he reasserted control over his emotions.

Slow down troop, or you'll get everyone killed.

Above, something pounded against one of the doors leading to the stairs. Jolie squeezed his shoulder, and Jaden wriggled about on his back. Gartrell stopped and leaned over the edge of the railing and peered down. Only two more flights to go.

"Let's pick it up a bit," he whispered to Jolie.

"I can't see a thing," she said.

"I can. Three steps to the next landing, turn left, down a flight, turn left, another flight, and then the door to—to what?"

"A hallway, and at the end of that, another door. Glass and mesh, like the one on Second Avenue."

Above, the pounding increased, and the moans of the dead reached their ears.

"Keep up with me," Gartrell said, and then he started down the steps at a good pace. Jolie hurried after him, her hand still on his shoulder. She stumbled down the steps but caught herself. In the process, she lost her grip on Gartrell's shoulder.

"Dave!" she said, her voice barely more than a whisper.

Gartrell turned at the next landing and looked up. She was at the top of the flight of stairs. Her hand was on the rail, and she looked right at him without seeing him.

"Come down. Twelve steps, just like in Alcoholics Anonymous. Take 'em quick, don't fuck around. You hear that racket upstairs? The dead'll be in here any minute. We gotta move, so shag it, lady."

She hurried down the steps, her left hand on the steel rail and the shotgun in her right. He reached out and took her shoulder when she made it to the landing and guided her around to the next flight of stairs.

"Another twelve steps, then the door. You see the light from under the door?"

"I see it!"

"Then hit it. Go!"

Keeping his hand on her shoulder this time, he followed her as she half-ran, half-stumbled down the steps. She almost fell against the door at the end of the stairwell, and her hand fumbled for the knob. Gartrell stopped her from opening it.

"Hold on. We'll do it like before—you open, I'll clear. Ready?"

"Ready."

Gartrell moved around her and ensured the wall was to Jaden's back and there was nothing that could harm him to the rear. Jaden seemed to be sleeping now, his head resting against Gartrell's shoulders. Gartrell wondered how that could be, as he must have been in some pain from the bonds on his wrists and ankles. He didn't dwell upon it. Instead, he flipped his NVGs up on their mount and readied the AA-12.

"Open it," he said.

Jolie pulled open the door, and filtered afternoon sunlight burst into the stairwell. It wasn't extremely bright, but Gartrell squinted against it anyway. He stepped into the hallway beyond. To his left, the hall ended at a closed elevator. To his right, it continued down toward a door that was three-quarters reinforced glass. Somewhere in the distance, he heard helicopters. Jaden stirred at the light, whining slightly. Gartrell waved Jolie into the hallway as he heard something give way upstairs. The dead had finally overwhelmed the door, and were doubtless streaming into the stairwell. Jolie hurried out, and Gartrell slammed the door shut. The darkness wouldn't cause the zeds much delay. Gravity would do its work, and they would find their way to the bottom, one way or another.

"Summit Six, Terminator Five. We're about to exit the building on Eighty-Sixth Street, and I'd estimate we're about a hundred meters east of the subway station. I can hear the helicopters, are they in firing position? Over." Through the glass door at the end of the hallway, Gartrell saw figures lurch past on the street outside.

"Terminator, Summit. They're ready whenever you are with nine hundred rounds of thirty mike-mike each. Flight of four hovering right close by, over."

"Six, we're ready. We are danger close and we need to get the hell out of here, so they should start sending rounds downrange right now, over." As he spoke, Gartrell heard sounds from behind the stairwell door. The stenches were finding their way down, and it sounded like half of them were falling down the stairs as opposed to walking down them.

"Dave..." Jolie looked toward the gray metal door, her shotgun in both hands. Sweat beaded on her upper lip, and thick strands of her red hair stuck to her face.

"Come on." Gartrell trotted toward the door, then stopped halfway down the hallway. He motioned for her to cover the exit, while he turned back toward the stairs.

"Terminator, Summit. Order out, party in ten, over."

It didn't take that long. Gartrell heard the helicopters shift position, and then the rotor noise was louder than before. Gartrell glanced over his shoulder and saw the zeds on the sidewalk outside slowly look up at the noise. He couldn't see the Apaches, but he hoped they were hovering above the buildings, not between them—

Loud cracking noises echoed through the concrete canyon outside as the Apaches opened up with their belly-mounted 30mm chainguns. At first, Gartrell didn't see much of anything happen, then the stenches right outside the door...*exploded.* It was as if they simply ceased to exist, transforming into disassociated body parts as the big high-explosive rounds utterly decimated anything soft and unprotected. The glass door cracked as metal fragments slammed into it, and Jolie jumped away from it and into Gartrell, jostling him.

"Jesus Christ!" she said over the sound of the helicopters and the firing guns.

"Not exactly, but the aviators would like to think so." Gartrell kept his AA-12 oriented on the stairwell door, and even above the discordant chaos breaking out on the street, he heard the sounds of the approaching zombie horde, stumbling their way down the steps. To no doubt they'd heard the helicopters as well, and were zeroing in on the sound.

"Terminator, Summit—Apaches report first pass complete, the block is temporarily clear if you want to make your exit, over."

"Roger that, Summit. We've got stenches to our rear, they'll be following us out in just a minute or so," Gartrell said as he pushed Jolie toward the door. Small shards of glass cracked beneath his boots. Jaden struggled suddenly, shouting. "Maybe if two of the gunships can start working on keeping the subway station entrance clear, the other two can guard the back door, over."

"Roger Terminator, will pass that on, over."

They made it to the door, and Jaden's struggles increased. Gartrell looked down at where the boy's wrists were bound to his body armor, and he saw the plastic quick ties had cut into his skin. He was bleeding, though not badly. He squeezed one of the boy's hands quickly, taking a moment to try and reassure him. It didn't work.

"It's going to be loud out there, so stay close!" Gartrell said to Jolie, having to raise his voice above Jaden's shouting and the thunder of the hovering helicopters. "The Apaches will give us some top cover, but they're not firing death rays—they can only stop what they hit, and their cannons are made to take out vehicles, not people. So stay close, and remember, keep them off us!"

"I will! I will!" Jolie looked at Jaden with a pained expression. "Oh, baby—" She reached past Gartrell's shoulder to touch her boy's face. Gartrell slapped her hand away.

"Later! Stay focused on what we have to do now! Let's move out!"

He pushed against the door, and it opened slowly. He looked down and saw why; the quivering remains of a zombie lay just outside. The ghoul had been blown into three different pieces, but its upper body was still moving, and the shredded remains of one arm slapped against the door, leaving blackened streaks of gore on the pitted metal. Its jaws opened and closed and its remaining eye rolled in its socket until it locked onto Gartrell. It stared at him hungrily, with a mindless malevolence that he felt would terrify even a Great White shark. He reached behind him and grabbed Jolie's arm, tugging her after him as he pushed the door open, sliding the thrashing corpse out of the way. Jaden's struggles increased, and Jolie spoke to him as comfortingly as she could over the din of the hovering helicopters.

Gartrell sidestepped the gory remains of the stenches that had been on the sidewalk. Above and behind their position, two AH-64D Apache Longbow attack helicopters hovered fifty feet above the buildings, their 30mm chainguns panning from left to right. Ahead, facing in the opposite direction on the other side of Second Avenue, another Apache bobbed in the breeze. Its chaingun barked as it fired on targets Gartrell couldn't see, zeds that were hidden by the billowing smoke of the burning cars.

Gee, if I'd known we'd be getting some close air support, I guess I could've saved my grenade.

"Come on!" Gartrell shouted over Jaden's shrieking and the pounding thud of rotor beats. He hurried up the sidewalk, stepping around body parts and puddles of gore. Many of the zombies that had been mutilated in the attack were still functioning, and they crawled toward him, trailing shattered limbs or in several cases, nothing more than coiled ropes of intestine. Gartrell was able to walk around them without shooting them. Ammunition was at a premium right now, and he knew he would have more opportunities to go to guns on any number of stenches in the near future.

"Oh my God!" Jolie cried, and Gartrell turned to find her staring at the shattered monstrosities that crept after them. "Oh, dear sweet *Jesus*!"

"Keep moving! Don't look at them, just keep moving!" As he spoke, Jaden suddenly began screaming. Gartrell turned and found a zombie advancing toward him in a crouch, its eyes fixed on him, its movements swift and certain. It wore a fireman's uniform, and one arm had been half-devoured. As it darted toward him, hissing, Gartrell took one step back and raised the AA-12. He had forgotten how surprisingly fast some of the dead could be.

One shot from the shotgun ensured it would no longer be a threat. The headless corpse collapsed to the street, black ichor shooting from the ragged stump of its neck.

Jared continued screaming and thrashed on Gartrell's back despite his bonds. Behind them, the two hovering Apaches opened up again as more zeds came around the corner of Second Avenue and East 86th Street. Even though they were hundreds of feet away, the roar of their chainguns was loud, even for Gartrell, who wore hearing protectors beneath his radio headset. For Jaden and Jolie, who only had cotton balls in their ears, it must have been ten times worse. The zombies disappeared into spreading explosions of body parts, asphalt from the street, and chunks of concrete and glass blown out of nearby building façades. The Apaches' cannons were fearsome weapons, but they were a little too imprecise for Gartrell's taste at the moment, which was why they were classified as 'area suppression weapons'—the guns kicked so hard that even the Apache itself rocked from side to side when firing.

Behind him, he heard Jolie's shotgun go off, and he looked over his shoulder. The zeds from the apartment building were free now, and they streamed into the street behind them. One of them—a runner—had taken off after Jolie, and she had dropped it with a blast from the .410. She hadn't killed it, however; the ghoul thrashed about on the ground, kicking the asphalt with its feet while flailing its hands in the air. Gartrell hadn't seen that kind of activity before; apparently, the zeds *could* be knocked down for the count by a severe enough head injury.

"Jolie, run!" Gartrell shouted. "Let the gunships take care of those things!" As he spoke, he waved to the hovering Apaches and pointed at the dozen or so zeds streaming toward them. The attack helicopters did as instructed, and a moment later, 30mm rounds were slashing through the zombies. Even as they were being cut down, the ghouls never gave any indication they knew they were under attack. They only had eyes for Gartrell, Jaden, and Jolie, and they continued to pursue them even after their legs had been blown into ribbons and their torsos disemboweled by the high explosive dual purpose rounds.

As they drew nearer to the cloud of dense black smoke that blew down Second Avenue, Gartrell slowed. Jaden had stopped struggling now, and he sagged against the first sergeant's back. Blood ran from his wrists where the plastic ties had pierced his flesh, and his struggles had only served to turn scrapes into ragged tears. Jolie stayed close behind them, and she fired her shotgun once again as a ghoul emerged from a shattered storefront—the Starbucks she and Gartrell had met in hours earlier.

"Uh, Terminator. This is Summit. Top cover says you're getting within sixty meters of the Second Avenue engagement area, and they can't suppress the zeds without maybe hitting you as well. What do you want to do? Over."

Gartrell looked at the intersection ahead and gauged that the smoke just wasn't heavy enough to adequately shield them. In fact, as he watched, several zombies strolled right through it. One of them was on fire. When they saw the humans, they hurried toward them as fast as their dead limbs could propel them. Gartrell checked behind him, and saw two other zeds were making their way up the sidewalk; an overhang prevented the Apache gunners from getting a visual on them, so they were unable to fire. One of the zombies crawled. The other hobbled.

"Jolie, shoot those things in the head once they're within twenty feet. Shoot the walker first, then wait for the crawler."

"All right."

"Summit, Terminator. I want the Apaches to use rockets on Second Avenue. I want them to light up the entire intersection and give us enough cover to make it into the subway without being detected. Can they do that for us right away? Over."

"Your call, Terminator. Stand by."

Gartrell raised the AA-12 and went to guns on the closest zombie, blasting its skull into fragments. It sank to the street like an empty plastic bag. Behind it, the ghoul that was on fire suddenly collapsed as well; the flames had consumed so much tissue that it couldn't walk any longer. Behind him, Jolie's shotgun cracked once. As Gartrell waited for the rest of the zombies ahead to get closer, he pulled his pistol and thumbed off the safety. Holding it in both hands, he carefully dispatched all the oncoming zeds with perfectly-placed headshots.

Five rounds out of the pistol, two out of the shotty.

"Terminator, Summit. Party in ten seconds, top cover recommends you pull back immediately while they do their thing, over."

Gartrell holstered his pistol and grabbed Jolie as she sighted on the zombie crawling up 86th Street. He ran back the way they had come, dragging her along behind. She squeaked as they passed the zombie crawling in the street and it reached out for her with one filthy hand. Flies buzzed around the dirty, bloodstained corpse.

"Where are we going? The subway station is back *there!*" Jolie said.

Her question was answered from above when a hissing roar cut through the air. Gartrell looked up to see one of the Apaches surrounded momentarily by flame and smoke as 2.75-inch rockets spat from the outboard pods slung beneath the attack helicopter's stubby wings. The rockets flew for less than a second before they slammed into the intersection at speeds approaching 400 miles an hour. They detonated the instant the point-contact fuses at the tip of each warhead made contact with something solid, and 17 pounds of high explosives ripped at dead flesh, automotive sheet metal, asphalt, and concrete again and again. Windows shattered and the faces of every building on the block cracked and crazed as each explosion yielded a strong shock wave that ripped through the intersection. Gartrell spun around and faced the devastation, not because he wanted to see it, but because he wanted to shield Jaden from any debris which might come hurtling their way.

The attack ended after just a few seconds, and the first helicopter super-elevated, climbing away at full power as the second Apache slid into its firing position. Thirty-eight high explosive rockets had laid the intersection to waste, and Gartrell looked up to see flames leaping almost a hundred feet into the air, flames that gave off voluminous clouds of thick, black smoke. Even from more than a hundred feet away, he felt the heat of the blaze on his body. The single Apache had done more damage in its attack than the main gun of the Coast Guard cutter *Escanaba* had during a similar attack Gartrell had witnessed the night before.

But through the inferno, zombies still moved. They walked through the flames and the dense smoke as if the conflagration didn't exist. Some of them were almost shredded from shrapnel and the effects of the explosions; others were blackened by the heat or actually aflame themselves. Many finally stumbled and collapsed, cooked by the fantastic heat, but others continued marching on, heading toward Gartrell and the others.

"Dave!"

Jolie's voice was distant, far away. Gartrell turned and looked behind them. More zombies advanced up 86th Street, coming in from the east, doubtless lured in by the hovering helicopters and explosions.

And then the second Apache unleashed its salvo of rockets, and the firestorm in the intersection doubled, then trebled. The shock waves raced down the street, flattening the zeds that had managed to survive the first attack. Jaden had screamed himself hoarse by now, and Gartrell grabbed one of his hands in a vain attempt to calm him. There was just no way that was happening. Gartrell thought it would be a miracle if the poor kid would be able to calm down in several weeks. The Apache hovering in the sky behind them actually drifted backwards. Gartrell grabbed Jolie's hand and pulled her to her feet.

"Come on, we gotta go now! That Apache, he's lining up on the zeds coming from the east, and we need to get out of here!"

"But what about the fire?" she asked, pointing to the raging inferno that waited for them in the intersection. The heat and flames were so intense that even the zombies hadn't survived it; they were blackened husks of sizzling, necrotic flesh lying strewn about. Those that still moved were so badly damaged that they were no longer a top threat.

Those closing in from the rear were a different story.

"Well, if we stay, we'll be in *his* zone of fire, and that's going to be a hell of a lot worse!" Gartrell indicated the Apache, which had now repositioned itself. Over the river, another attack helicopter banked in and took position above and behind the first. "Come on!"

Without waiting for her to agree, he yanked her after him and ran like hell toward the intersection. As he did, he pulled a bottle of water from one of his cargo pockets and opened it. He doused Jaden's head with a liberal amount of liquid, then splashed the remainder on his face and BDUs and tossed the container to the gutter. He heard Jolie do the same, using one of the water bottles strapped to the side of the backpack.

At a hundred meters from the intersection, the air was noticeably hot.

At fifty meters, it was scalding, and Gartrell was happy he had splashed water all over himself and Jaden.

At twenty-five meters, the heat was almost blistering, and Gartrell found himself taking brief, shallow breaths. The smoke was thick and cloying, and visibility was diminishing. On his back, Jaden was wracked by a coughing fit.

At ten meters from the subway entrance, Gartrell's uniform felt like it was on fire and that his skin was burning beneath it. Something wet and hot landed on him, and he realized it was Jolie, showering her son with the contents of another bottle of water. The liquid sizzled when it hit the scorching hot pavement. The asphalt was already melting in places, and Gartrell hopped onto the concrete sidewalk as he bolted for the stairs leading into the subway station. Behind him, he heard the Apache's chaingun open up again, barely audible above the roar of the flames. The air was toxic, and it burned Gartrell's throat and made his eyes sting and water. The green paint on the metal barrier surrounding the stairs leading to the underground subway was melting. Jaden's screams were lost in the unholy cacophony of hell as Gartrell made it to the stairs and stumbled down them. Halfway down, he realized it wasn't Jaden who was screaming. It was Gartrell himself.

Below, the darkness was cooler, inviting. Gartrell plunged into it, grateful for the sudden change in temperature that seemed to be almost wintery compared to the hell above. He stopped at the foot of the stairs and looked back as Jolie staggered down the steps. She had lost the shotgun, and her hair was smoldering. She coughed and retched, almost doubled over. Her footing was unsure, and she slowed as she entered the darkness, gasping for breath.

And then Jaden screamed. Gartrell sensed movement in the blackness behind him, and he cursed himself for forgetting where he was, what he was doing, what the real threat was. He snapped his night vision goggles down over his eyes and turned, his right hand already closing around the AA-12's pistol-grip, his index finger sliding onto the trigger. The NVGs exited their standby mode and powered up, and what had been pure, unbroken blackness to his unaided vision came alive in ghostly green hues.

To the zombies, Gartrell and Jaden were presented as silhouettes against the light filtering down the stairway from above, and they launched themselves forward like cheetahs sprinting after their prey. The first was so close to Gartrell that it almost grabbed him before the first blast from the AA-12 blew it back, ripping through its chest and decimating a cardiopulmonary system it no longer needed. His second shot beheaded it, and he did the same to the next four ghouls as they surged toward him. It was over within seconds, and Gartrell crept over the now-motionless corpses and approached the trio of turnstiles and a larger exit designed for use by the disabled. He started to reach for the latter's push-bar release, but then he noticed the alarm system on the door; he had no doubt it was battery-powered, and the last thing he wanted was for an alarm to start shrieking in the darkness.

Well, not that the gunshots probably went unnoticed…

He stepped back from the door and reached into one of the pockets on his body armor. He found an infrared chemlight and bent it in the center. It made a snapping sound, and through the NVGs, it was as if someone had just turned on a floodlight. Gartrell hurled the inch-and-a-half device into the subway tunnel.

The additional illumination made the NVGs even more effective, as they could read into the lower levels of the infrared bandwidth. The tunnel seemed clear, but a scuffling sound caught his attention, and he looked to his right, to the north. Zeds leapt off the opposing platform and shuffled across the southbound tunnel, attracted by the brief, one-sided firefight. They stumbled about in the darkness, and without the light pouring from the stairwell behind him, they were completely blind.

"Dave." Jolie coughed and spat. Gartrell turned to her, and she pointed up the stairway with her revolver, which she held in both hands. "They're coming." A trail of blood ran down one side of her face, and he figured something had sliced open her scalp, probably a piece of shrapnel. He moved grabbed her arm without even bothering to raise his NVGs and glance upward. He knew the zeds would follow them down, despite the raging inferno that blazed away over their heads.

"Zombies in the tunnel, but they can't see us. Stay quiet, and let me lead you. We have to hop over some turnstiles, and then we're going to walk up the platform to the right. You understand me?"

"Yes. Jaden's so scared—"

"So am I. Do as I tell you. You go first, then turn and help me and Jaden across." He led her to the turnstiles and helped her climb over one. She was unsteady, and her movements were furtive, unsure. He wanted to yell at her, but he didn't dare, not with the zeds so close. They were already zeroing in on their position, and their moans echoed in the empty subway tunnel. Jolie looked about wildly, but in the inky blackness she could see nothing. Gartrell slapped her shoulder as he heaved himself over the turnstile, and she grabbed his arm and helped him across. It was tough going, especially while carrying all manner of weapons and with a forty-pound kid strapped to his back, but Gartrell made it.

And just in time, for the first of the ghouls made it to their platform and hoisted itself onto it. A single shot from Gartrell's AA-12 sent its headless body flying back onto the northbound tracks. That only served to attract the rest of the zeds in the tunnel, and they rushed toward their position. Gartrell grabbed Jolie's arm and pulled her after him, hurrying down the platform. As he did, he spoke quietly into his headset's boom microphone.

"Summit Six, Terminator. We're in the tunnel—we made it. Hats off to the aviators, they got us through, over."

The response from the 2/87th's commander was broken up by static, and Gartrell had to concentrate to make out the words. "Terminator, Summit. Your transmission is breaking up, we can barely get you. Confirm you're in the tunnels, over."

"Summit, Terminator is in the tunnel, over."

The response was awash with static and an oscillating tone. They were already too far underground for the radio to work properly. Jaden moaned, and the ghouls behind the group caught the sound and stumbled after them. One of stenches fell right off the edge of the platform and slammed onto the tracks with enough force to break bones, but it struggled back to its feet and continued on, dragging one leg behind it. Gartrell led Jolie to the end of the platform, where a small gate bearing a DO NOT ENTER sign blocked off a maintenance ladder. He brought Jolie to a halt and pushed her against the wall.

"Stand right there. I'm going to have to thin out the herd a bit," he said.

"I can't see anything."

"Don't worry. I can. We're good, we've got about"—he looked over his shoulder at the oncoming zombies—"six or seven stenches to deal with, then we're going to go down a ladder and head up the tunnel. Stay cool, Jolie. We're getting through this."

"Trying," she said. But the expression on her face said it all. She was already past her limit, and the only thing that kept her running was force of will and the love for her son.

"Stay right here," Gartrell told her. He did a quick visual reconnoiter of the area, and saw no zeds in the area other than those to their south. He stepped away from Jolie and walked back the way they came; this way, when the zeds keyed in on the AA-12's muzzle flashes, they wouldn't threaten Jolie directly.

Just me and poor little Jaden. That's the ticket, Gartrell—put a four-year-old in harm's way.

The zombies groped their way down the platform, moaning, hissing, their dead eyes rolling in their dry sockets as they struggled to separate shapes from the blanket of darkness that enshrouded them. Overhead, Gartrell heard the rotor beats of the Apaches fading into the distance. Their job done, the attack helicopters were retreating, probably to rearm, refuel, and repeat their attacks elsewhere.

He waited for the zeds to close on his position. Before he opened up, he checked over his shoulder to make sure Jolie was still secure; she was. He raised the AA-12 to his shoulder, sighted on the closest zed, and fired. It collapsed to the platform twenty feet from him. Jaden screamed at the sudden sound and struggled mightily, and his movements were so severe this time that Gartrell's second shot missed the next zed entirely. That gave it enough time to charge forward with a surprising burst of speed, and Gartrell dropped it when it was only four feet away. The rest of the stenches roared and hurried toward him as if of one, hands outstretched, jaws spread wide. It took all of Gartrell's discipline not to mash the AA-12's trigger down and rock and roll on full auto as he backpedaled, Jaden's screams in his ears as he fired again and again and again. Spent 12 gauge shotgun shells flew out of the weapon's ejector port and rolled across the platform floor as Gartrell faded back, leaving a trail of still corpses in his wake. When he was done, he had laid waste to seven zeds.

Across the tracks, more commotion from the other platform. And back at the turnstiles, a few more zeds that had survived the inferno overhead managed to make it to the platform. Gartrell counted at least twenty, maybe thirty zombies had entered the tunnel. He ejected the AA-12's ammunition drum, and found he had only three rounds left. He suppressed a curse and reached into his knapsack. He pulled out the other drum and extracted the three shotgun shells from it, then hurled it southbound as far as he was able. The drum bounced down the tracks, and the zombies turned toward the sound, peering into the darkness. Gartrell loaded the three shells into his remaining drum, then slapped it back into the AA-12. He now had a total of seven rounds left, and then the AA-12 would be useless.

Jaden moved on his back and whined loudly, doubtless from the pain emanating from his bleeding wrists. Gartrell winced at the sound as the stenches turned back in their direction. They started moving immediately, casting about in the darkness for the prey they knew was there. Gartrell fell back to Jolie and touched her wrist. She started and brought up her revolver.

"It's me," Gartrell whispered. "We're leaving. Right now." He grabbed her wrist and led her to the maintenance gate. It was unlocked, so he pushed it open. Below was a short ladder, only three or four rungs which led to the tunnel's surface. No stenches were in the immediate vicinity, so he brought his lips close to Jolie's ear. She stank of sweat, grime, and singed hair.

"Three steps to the bottom. You go first. I'll move you into position, but be quick about it—we're danger close here, the stenches are closing in."

"Okay."

He had her place the revolver in her jacket pocket, and then maneuvered her so she stood at the edge of the platform. After he positioned her hands on the ladder's rails, she quickly descended down the short ladder. Once on the ground below, she pressed her back against the wall and waited. Gartrell went down the ladder as carefully as he could, struggling not to make any noise—the first of the zeds was only twenty feet away at the most. The barrel of the AA-12 struck one of the handrails with a metallic clang, and the nearest zombie charged straight ahead. It slammed face-first into the wall next to the ladder and bounced off with a grunt. As it sprawled across the platform floor, Gartrell had the surprisingly strong urge to laugh at it.

He reached out and took Jolie's wrist again and led her into the tunnel, panning his head from left to right as he scanned for any sign of additional danger. So far, the tunnel ahead looked vacant, though even the NVGs could expose only so much—there was close to zero illumination, and even the night vision goggles needed some source of light to amplify. Behind them, bodies hit the ground as the zeds on the platform walked right off it and crashed onto the subway tracks. Gartrell looked back. Several of them survived the tumble pretty much intact, and they rose to their feet and resumed the hunt. Some were disoriented, and actually started moving across the tunnel, or heading back in the direction they came from—

Something fell over in the darkness to his right, and Gartrell turned toward the southbound tunnel. He shouted a curse when he saw literally *dozens* of stenches pushing their way through the man-sized openings in the wall that separated the northbound tracks from the southbound one. Some of the zeds were only feet away.

Gartrell fired, dropping three of the zombies closest to them instantly. He blew the leg off another, and a fourth he blasted back with a shot to its chest. Jaden came alive on his back, writhing and screaming, and Gartrell's fifth shot missed its target entirely, and the sixth only decimated one of its shoulders. Undeterred by the gruesome damage, the ghoul lurched toward him, flailing about in the darkness with its one good arm. It missed Gartrell by inches, and the first sergeant unslung his AA-12 and swung it at the zombie's head with all his strength. The blow knocked the stench to the deck, but another one sprang up to take its place as Gartrell cast the AA-12 aside and ripped his MP5 from its tactical truss. Holding it in one hand, he clicked off the safety and ripped off a burst, moving the submachine gun from right to left. It was mostly a waste of ammunition, but the sudden fusillade of nine millimeter rounds knocked the zeds back a few paces, giving him the opening he needed. He grabbed Jolie's arm in his left hand and yanked her away from the wall. He took off at a run, heading north, as she stumbled along after him. She made little noises in her throat, but Gartrell was certain the zeds behind couldn't hear them; they must have been deafened by the gunfire, and their own moans filled the subway tunnel with a creepy, ululating cacophony. Jaden continued writhing on Gartrell's back, whimpering as he bounced up and down in time with the soldier's gait.

Behind them, he heard the dead as they surged up the tunnel in pursuit. Ahead, two more zeds appeared, crossing over from the southbound tracks. Gartrell fired on the move, three shots resulting in two fatal hits—a terrible ratio, given his current ammunition state. The walls of the tunnel were coated with a grayish material that he presumed was some sort of fireproofing. It seemed to capture what little illumination there was in the tunnel. Gartrell made Jolie grab onto his belt—it took more time than it should have, but he couldn't speak—then he fished around in his pocket for another infrared chemlight. He found it, activated it, and hurled it down the tunnel before them. Light blossomed through the NVGs, and he saw the remainder of the northbound tunnel was clear…but in the distance, at the very edge of the goggles' acuity, he thought he saw some sort of obstruction.

Jesus, what the fuck could that be?

And then, more zombies crossed over from the southbound tracks. They stumbled through the darkness, completely blind, but they sensed the activity in the tunnel, and that activity meant there was a chance at finding food.

Jaden struggled again, and Gartrell moved forward, heading for the zombies ahead. He knew the light infantry troops were in that direction, and if he could do anything to close the gap, then that was what he would do.

"Jolie, stay with me," he whispered over his shoulder. "If you drop behind, they'll get you."

"I know." Her voice was more whimper than whisper. "If anything happens to me, take care of my son."

"Roger that."

Gartrell advanced toward the zombies milling about ahead, pulling ahead of the stenches to the rear. Their footfalls were as quiet as possible, but he doubted the zeds could tell the difference between their steps and their own. As he closed on the group, he made sure his last magazine of MP5 ammunition was where it was supposed to be—he would need it in a hurry. It was. He shouldered the weapon and took aim at the zombie closest to him, about thirty feet away. It stared unblinking into the darkness, as stupid as a fire hydrant and about half as good looking.

The quick tie binding Jaden's left ankle to him failed suddenly, and the boy shifted crazily on his back. He cried out as the pain in his wrists doubtless doubled. Jolie grabbed him, tried to keep him steady, but the young boy screamed and thrashed, his voice hoarse and dry, but still it echoed throughout the tunnel. The zombies ahead of them turned to the south as if of one mind, and they rushed toward them as fast as they were able. Then one of them went down, tripping in the darkness; the rest of the stenches piled up on the first, falling like a line of dominoes.

Gartrell pulled his knife and cut the quick ties that bound Jaden to him. "Jolie, grab Jaden and move to the right—flatten against the wall there! Keep him out of the way, then get the flashlight out of your pack. Don't turn it on, just let me know when you've got it!" he said as Jaden slipped off his back. He held on to the boy's left wrist, preventing him from collapsing to the ground. If that happened, he didn't want Jolie fishing around in the darkness trying to find him. "Do you have him?"

He felt Jolie tug Jaden away. "I have him! We're moving to the wall!" He heard her shrug off the backpack, and it hit the ground next to the wall.

Gartrell shouldered the MP5 and blasted two zeds through the head, dropping them as they rose to their feet. He then turned at the waist and fired at the mass of zombies behind them. He dropped one zed, then another, the nine millimeter projectiles blasting furrows through their skulls. He turned back to the north and fired again, one round per stench, firing with a quick precision that belied the near-panic that nibbled at the edges of his discipline and threatened to overwhelm him. If that happened, then they would all die.

And Gartrell wasn't ready to die just yet.

Especially when a lady and her autistic son were depending on him.

So the zombies fell to the rails like clockwork. Every shot he fired resulted in a bullet punching through a stench's skull, turning the remains of its brain into something like watery oatmeal, and blasting a good portion of that goo out the other side as the bullet continued on its merry way. He counted off the shots as he went, even though he didn't know how many rounds were still in the magazine after he had ripped off on full auto earlier.

One.

Two.

Three.

Four.

Five.

Six.

Seven.

Eight.

Once he had created a buffer zone between himself and the zombies to the north, he turned and engaged those rolling up on them from the rear. They were close, much closer than he had expected them to be, only fifteen feet from where Jolie crouched over Jaden. She hugged her screaming son to her chest with one arm, her lips pressed against the top of his head as she rooted through the backpack with her other hand. Gartrell dropped the leading zed as it lurched toward them, zeroing in on Jaden's cries.

Nine.

Ten.

Eleven.

Twelve.

Thirteen.

Fourteen.

The MP5 ran dry then, and Gartrell ejected the spent magazine and slammed the new one into the weapon. He yanked back on the cocking lever and cycled a round into the chamber and resumed firing.

One.
Two.
Three.
Four.
Five.

"I have the flashlight!" Jolie said.

"Turn it on and shine it at them, both sides of the tunnel! Make sure those fuckers see it!"

She did as he instructed her to without hesitation. The zombies blinked at the sudden bright light, their dead pupils slowly narrowing to pinpoints. But when they charged forward, emboldened by the light, Jolie cried out in horror.

"Shit, now what?" she screamed as Gartrell continued firing.

"Throw it across the tracks! Throw it *now!*"

Jolie pitched the metal Maglite toward the southbound tracks, and the bright flashlight tumbled through the air end over end. It sailed through one of the openings in the barrier wall and came to a rest on the other set of tracks, its bright beam shining into the gloom. The zombies all turned to watch it travel, and then they moved after it.

Just like with the flare...they associate the light with food!

Yet some hung back. Either they didn't fall for the trick, or Jaden's whimpering was a stronger indicator that a hot meal was very nearby. These remaining zombies, perhaps twelve in all, closed in on them ahead and behind. Gartrell clenched his teeth. This wasn't working out. The second he started firing again, the shots would only recall those who had crossed over to the other side of the tracks.

For an instant, an inelegant solution presented itself: he could slip past the encroaching zombies, and leave them to make their way to Jolie and her son, while he made his escape.

Not happening.

"Jolie, get ready to move—they're still closing in on us. We're going to advance. Leave the pack, just grab Jaden, and get ready."

And with that, Gartrell resumed firing, blasting away at the zombies in front of them, methodically cutting them down. He scanned to his left and saw the rest of the horde hovered around the shining flashlight, but now they looked up, the MP5's stroboscopic muzzle flashes capturing their attention.

Behind him, Jolie screamed.

Gartrell spun around, and Jolie shoved Jaden toward him as a zombie grabbed her from behind. Gartrell grabbed Jaden's arm with one hand as Jolie pulled her revolver and fired over her shoulder, right into the zombie's face. It fell away from her, but pulled her down with it. She screamed again as she fell to the railroad ties between the rails, and before Gartrell could move to assist her, another zombie fell upon her.

"Jolie!"

"*Save Jaden, save Jaden!*" she shouted, and then her words turned into a shriek as another zombie landed upon her and its teeth found her flesh. The revolver cracked again and again beneath the writhing mass of bodies, but it was too late for that. Gartrell fired twice into the pile, and hoped the bullets ended Jolie's life before the zombies took it from her.

"Momma!" Jaden cried. "Momma-Momma-Momma!"

Gartrell snatched the boy up in one arm and turned back to the north. A stench lunged for him, and he fired two rounds through its face, then turned sideways as it fell past him. Another zombie loomed before him. Gartrell killed it. Jaden screamed and thrashed in his arm, calling out for his mother, again and again. Gartrell continued to advance, firing. But Jaden was ruining his accuracy; two rounds missed taking down a zombie, and he had to waste a third to finish it off. He missed the next ghoul entirely, and didn't zero it until it was within arm's reach. When it fell to the railroad ties before him, its ruined skull bounced off his boots.

God, I'm losing it…

"Term…inder One…your pos…"

The fragmented message over his radio buoyed his spirits immediately. "Pathfinder, this is Terminator! I'm in the tunnel, moving northbound toward what looks to be a stalled subway train, over!" As he spoke, Gartrell kept moving, bobbing and weaving past the zombies now. He just wasn't able to shoot all of them. Something brushed across his back, and he spun to find a ghoul standing *right there*, so close he had to swing the MP5 at its head to push it back far enough from him that he could shoot it. Which he did, and the zombie collapsed to an unmoving heap.

And then the MP5 was empty.

Gartrell threw the weapon at advancing zombies and pulled his pistol. He had fired five times.

Which meant he had eight rounds left in the magazine.

He had to put Jaden down, and he pushed him against the wall, pinning him there with his body. He pulled his final magazine of .45 caliber ammunition for the pistol from his pocket and discharged the weapon, taking out eight zombies in less than five seconds. The slide locked in the open position when the weapon ran empty. Gartrell ejected the magazine, slammed in the fresh one, and thumbed the slide release, sending the first round into the chamber as a stench slammed into him. It sank its teeth into his armor's shoulder strap and dug in with its legs, dragging him away from the wall with surprising strength. Gartrell shouted and pounded on its head with the butt of the pistol, but it made no difference; the zed hung on like a dog clenching its most favored chew toy between its jaws. It shook its head from side to side, and Gartrell wound up wrapping his left arm around it, just to hold it in place. He extended his arm and dropped a zombie that moved to join the fracas. They were so close now that they didn't need any light to see. They knew food was so very near.

Gartrell fired again and again, the Mk 23 pistol kicking hard in his hand. He shouted over the radio for the infantry platoon, but received no response he could fully comprehend. It seemed the unit was close, but not close enough to count. Gartrell kept firing, and the bodies kept stacking up.

And then he was down to two rounds.

In the darkness, Jaden screamed.

Gartrell punched the zombie hanging onto his body armor full in the jaw, fracturing it. The ghoul finally fell away, rolling across the railroad ties. Gartrell evaded another zed by ducking past it. More stenches surrounded Jaden, his cries drawing them to him like bees to honey. There were so many, too many. And more swam in the darkness around Gartrell, circling, trying to locate him now that the shooting had stopped. Gartrell looked at Jaden as the small boy kept crying for his mother, his eyes wide in the darkness, the tears pouring down his beautiful face, his copper hair matted with sweat and grime. The boy's last few moments would be spent in absolute terror, terror that would be all he knew before guttural agony set in as the stenches set about their work. Gartrell felt a heavy sadness descend upon him. Only seven feet separated them.

Gartrell found himself mentally reciting the Lord's Prayer, and a small measure of peace came to him.

Our Father who art in heaven, hallowed be thy name.
Thy kingdom come.
Thy will be done on earth as it is in heaven.

Give us this day our daily bread, and forgive us our trespasses, as we forgive those who trespass against us, and lead us not into temptation, but deliver us from evil.

"Jaden," he called, raising the pistol. "Jaden, baby. It's okay. It's okay."

Jaden heard his voice, and he calmed a bit, looking through the darkness, trying to find Gartrell. His hands were bloodied from the rents cut into his wrists, and he had small bloody handprints on his seared denim jacket. The zombies swung toward Gartrell's voice, just as he had hoped they would. He aimed the pistol at Jaden, and time seemed to dilate in a way he had never fully experienced before, even when he was in the full heat of combat where every moment stretched out over the course of an hour. As he lined up the pistol's sights on Jaden's small head, he had a sudden premonition, the sudden *idea* that this is what McDaniels had felt so long ago in Afghanistan, when the two of them were the leaders of PHANTOM Team, and they had wrestled with a horrible decision: to kill an unarmed boy who had discovered them, so that he couldn't warn others and bring the Taliban upon them. Gartrell had supported the execution, out of sheer military necessity. And he would have carried it out as well. But the decision was not his to make. McDaniels had wrestled with the choice for as long as he could, but in the end, his morality overcame his discipline. While Gartrell had always known that was what happened, he had never fully appreciated it until now. First Sergeant David Gartrell had seen combat in every war and participated in scores of clandestine operations, where many people met violent ends. He had seen utter brutality up close, and had managed not to participate in the worst of it, but there was still some blood on his hands.

And here he was, confronted with circumstances that demanded a specific outcome: that he execute a small boy to save him from an even more heinous end.

And he couldn't do it.

A zombie seized Jaden's shoulder finally with a hissing roar, and it bent toward him. Gartrell adjusted his aim and put a bullet through its head as Jaden screamed yet again, the terror returning. The rest of the zeds whirled, their ranks split—half turned toward Gartrell, half turned upon the screaming young boy who never truly understood what was happening. He only wanted the comfort of his mother.

He would never have that comfort, ever again.

So Gartrell reached deep inside himself and found the strength to act, to give the boy the only comfort he could. His last round made Jaden's small head seem to explode, and the child's body wilted to the bottom of the subway tunnel where it was trampled by the zombies as they turned toward the rangy first sergeant. Gartrell pulled his knife.

"Come on, you stupid sacks of shit," he said. His voice was small amidst the moans of the dead, practically lost in the flood of sound. He had failed to protect the woman and the boy, had failed to accomplish even a mission as basic as that, and now his time was up. No more options left, just fight and die.

The subway tunnel was filled by fire and thunder, and Gartrell's NVGs overloaded as something exploded nearby, something that burned bright and loud for a moment or two before disappearing, as if a camera flash had gone off in the darkness. A cascading series of cracks assaulted his ears, even through the radio headset and the hearing protectors beneath it, and long ribbons of fire spat out at the stenches. Their heads exploded, and in some instances their bodies just *disintegrated*, as if they had been hit by some sort of death ray. Gartrell watched all of this with a detached, remote interest as well as he could; his goggles kept overloading, and the racket was so loud and vicious he couldn't even think properly. He just stood where he was, even as a zed reached toward him with grimy hands, its jaws spread wide, its tongue black and swollen, maggots pouring from one eye socket, its hair singed away and the skin on its face and scalp blackened, as if by some incredible heat. Just as it touched him, something cracked again, and the zed pitched over onto its right side at Gartrell's feet. He saw a small hole in the side of its head.

Beyond the corpse lay Jaden, and Gartrell's eyes burned with sudden tears when he saw the tiny boy. He lay on his back, his forehead pushed slightly inward; the back of his skull had been blown away. His cranium looked deflated, irregular beneath his beautiful hair. His alabaster skin was almost white through the NVGs, and his eyes were closed, as if he had fallen asleep. His lips were slightly parted, and Gartrell knew what the boy's last words had been.

Momma...Momma...Momma...

Gartrell walked to the small corpse and sank to his knees beside it, his chest on fire. Tears streamed down his face as he picked up Jaden and held him close, ignoring the ropy mass of matter that dangled from behind the boy's ears. He just held the body to him and wept, shutting out all else, tuning out the death and devastation that raged all around him.

And finally, even that came to an end. Gartrell became aware of someone talking to him, someone kneeling right next to him. A hand gripped his arm and shook him roughly, and Jaden's head turned away from Gartrell's chest. He fully saw the damage his round had done for the first time.

Dear God, you fucking cheat, you fucking piece of shit, how could you let this happen to someone who couldn't even fucking understand *what was going down?*

"Hey guy—hey first sergeant, you all right?" Someone shook Gartrell again, and he slowly looked to his right. A young second lieutenant knelt beside him, peering at Gartrell through his own night vision goggles. His face covered with beard stubble and sweat-streaked grime. He clutched an M4 carbine against his chest. Behind him, another soldier stood. This one carried a bulky Squad Automatic Weapon, the M249 SAW. Gartrell looked around. More soldiers had taken defensive positions in the gloom. They carried a variety of weapons, all standard issue, nothing esoteric like his AA-12. These were regular Army soldiers, and from their shoulder patches they were with the 10th Mountain Division (Light Infantry). The platoon Gartrell had been trying to link up with. The lightfighters had finally arrived.

Two seconds after he had shot a small toddler named Jaden.

Two seconds.

The platoon commander was saying something else when Gartrell refocused on him. "Where the fuck were you?" he asked. His voice was tight and dry, as full of emotion as a desert was filled with water.

"What's that, first sergeant?"

Gartrell didn't raise his voice. He didn't need to. He knew how to get a point across with screaming and yelling, and he reached inside himself and pulled it out one word at a time, nice and easy and full of barbs. "Where. The. *Fuck*. Were. You."

The second lieutenant facing him got the message loud and clear, and he looked down at the tiny corpse in Gartrell's lap as if for the first time. "Uh...this tunnel is blocked by a subway train...we had to move through the other tunnel...and then we, you know, we had to get set up. We had to protect ourselves too..."

Gartrell pushed Jaden's body into the officer's arms. The lightfighter recoiled and tried to pull away, but Gartrell's hand lashed out and caught him behind the neck and held him in place. "You did a great job practicing force protection, lieutenant. Looks to me like all your guys made it. All the guys with the guns are still standing, and zed's down for the count. But look down. Look down at this four-year-old boy and ask yourself: should I have moved a bit faster?"

"I don't need this shit from you—!"

"Shut up, butter bars." Gartrell rose to his feet and glared down at the lieutenant through his night vision goggles. "Look down at that boy. Remind yourself who you are, what you do, and who you're supposed to fucking protect." He looked up at the rest of the soldiers and found none of them could withstand the weight of his gaze; they all looked away and concentrated on their prearranged fire lanes. Gartrell looked down as the lieutenant gently placed Jaden's body on the railroad ties that connected the rails and rose to his feet.

"I'm sorry," was all he said.

"Not interested. Give me a weapon, lieutenant."

"Why?"

Gartrell looked past the lieutenant's shoulder as the troops arrayed to their south stirred uneasily. In the distance, the moans of the dead echoed in the subway tunnel.

"Because the dead are coming, lieutenant. And they're hungry. They're always, *always* hungry."

END

AFTERWORD

So the question has been raised: Why a novella, and not a full-on sequel to *The Gathering Dead*?

Let me explain, and allow me to get the more pressing business out of the way first. Yes, there were will be a sequel to *The Gathering Dead*, and it will be called *The Rising Horde*. McDaniels and company will be back, along with a cast of new folks as they engage the rising legions of the dead in that good old military-on-zombie action that so many people crave. And there will be additional dimensions covered in the sequel, such as how the United States fares, as well as some international goings-on that will need to be checked on. I am working to try and deliver the book by Fall 2011.

Now, as far as the novella is concerned…

I just wasn't finished with New York City falling to the dead, and I believe I hinted at that in the conclusion of *The Gathering Dead*. While there wasn't a great deal left over, it didn't belong in the first book. And to me, it doesn't belong in the next one either. So a novella was the best way to accommodate the material, without causing an overrun in the first book and a "what the fuck?" moment in the sequel. Plus, I wanted to work on Gartrell a bit more. I wanted to give the character a challenge he really wasn't ready for, and I wanted him to discover that he's not some near-omnipotent war god. His successes depend on his skills, his prowess, his knowledge…and a liberal dose of luck, something that he runs out of here.

I hope you'll agree.

The usual round of thank yous are required here: fellow writer Fred Anderson for being a good sport about the whole thing and for getting me his comments lightning-fast. Joe Lebert for his input as well. Derek Paterson for his detailed analysis of everything that went right and wrong. And Mike Costa for the sanity check—I'll try not to destroy your boat when I come down to Jawja see you.

And of course, the biggest thanks go to you, the readers. Without you, this would be nothing more than a solitary exercise. Thanks for the all the support, ideas, and yes, the criticism. The more I get, the better off the next project will be. Keep it comin', gang!

THE GATHERING DEAD WILL RETURN IN
THE RISING HORDE
FALL 2011

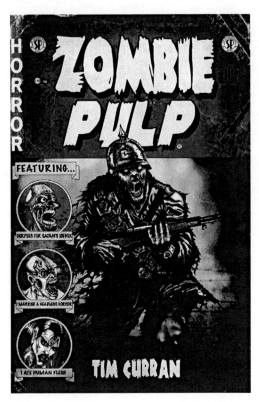

ZOMBIE PULP

Tim Curran
Dead men tell tales.
From the corpse factories
of World War I
where graveyard rats
sharpen their teeth on
human bones to the wind-
blown cemeteries of the
prairie where resurrection
comes at an unspeakable
price...from the compound
of a twisted messianic cult
leader and his army of
zombies to a post-
apocalyptic wasteland
where all that stands
between the living and the
evil dead is sacrifice in the
form of a lottery.

Dead men do tell tales. And these are their stories.
Zombie Pulp is a collection of 9 short stories and 2 never before
published novellas from the twisted undead mind of
Tim Curran..

WHITE FLAG OF THE DEAD
Joseph Talluto

**Book 1
Surrender of
the Living.**

Millions died when the Enillo Virus swept the earth. Millions more were lost when the victims of the plague refused to stay dead, instead rising to slay and feed on those left alive. For survivors like John Talon and his son Jake, they are faced with a choice: Do they submit to the dead, raising the white flag of surrender? Or do they find the will to fight, to try and hang on to the last shreds or humanity?

Surrender of the Living is the first high octane installment in the White Flag of the Dead series.

RESURRECTION
By Tim Curran
www.corpseking.com

The rain is falling and the dead are rising. It began at an ultra-secret government laboratory. Experiments in limb regeneration-an unspeakable union of Medieval alchemy and cutting edge genetics result in the very germ of horror itself: a gene trigger that will reanimate dead tissue...any dead tissue. Now it's loose. It's gone viral. It's in the rain. And the rain has not stopped falling for weeks. As the country floods and corpses float in the streets, as cities are submerged, the evil dead are rising. And they are hungry.

"I REALLY love this book...Curran is a wonderful storyteller who really should be unleashed upon the general horror reading public sooner rather than later." – *DREAD CENTRAL*

Available at www.severedpress.com, Amazon and most online bookstores

DEMONMACHY
Brant Danay

As the universe slowly dies, all demonkind is at war in a tournament of genocide. The prize? Nirvana. The Necrodelic, a death addict who smokes the flesh of his victims as a drug, is determined to win this afterlife for himself. His quest has taken him to the planet Grystiawa, and into a duel with a dream-devouring snake demon who is more than he seems. Grystiawa has also been chosen as the final battleground in the ancient spider-serpent wars. As armies of arachnid monstrosities and ophidian gladiators converge upon the planet, the Necrodelic is forced to choose sides in a cataclysmic combat that could well prove his demise. Beyond Grystiawa, a Siamese twin incubus and succubus, a brain-raping nightmare fetishist, a gargantuan insect queen, and an entire universe of genocidal demons are forming battle plans of their own. Observing the apocalyptic carnage all the while is Satan himself, watching voyeuristically from the very Hell in which all those who fail will be damned to eternal torment. Who will emerge victorious from this cosmic armageddon? And what awaits the victor beyond the blood-drenched end of time? The battle begins in Demonmachy. Twisting Satanic mythologies and Eastern religions into an ultraviolent grotesque nightmare, the Messiah of Death Saga will rip your eyeballs right out of your skull. Addicted to its psychedelic darkness, you'll immediately sew and screw and staple and weld them back into their sockets so you can read more. It's an intergalactic, interdimensional harrowing that you'll never forget...and may never recover from.

Available at www.severedpress.com, Amazon and most online bookstores

The Official Zombie Handbook: Sean T Page

Since pre-history, the living dead have been among us, with documented outbreaks from ancient Babylon and Rome right up to the present day. But what if we were to suffer a zombie apocalypse in the UK today? Through meticulous research and field work, The Official Zombie Handbook (UK) is the only guide you need to make it through a major zombie outbreak in the UK, including: -Full analysis of the latest scientific information available on the zombie virus, the living dead creatures it creates and most importantly, how to take them down - UK style. Everything you need to implement a complete 90 Day Zombie Survival Plan for you and your family including home fortification, foraging for supplies and even surviving a ghoul siege. Detailed case studies and guidelines on how to battle the living dead, which weapons to use, where to hide out and how to survive in a country dominated by millions of bloodthirsty zombies. Packed with invaluable information, the genesis of this handbook was the realisation that our country is sleep walking towards a catastrophe - that is the day when an outbreak of zombies will reach critical mass and turn our green and pleasant land into a grey and shambling wasteland. Remember, don't become a cheap meat snack for the zombies!

BIOHAZARD

Tim Curran

The day after tomorrow: Nuclear fallout. Mutations. Deadly pandemics. Corpse wagons. Body pits. Empty cities. The human race trembling on the edge of extinction. Only the desperate survive. One of them is Rick Nash. But there is a price for survival: communion with a ravenous evil born from the furnace of radioactive waste. It demands sacrifice. Only it can keep Nash one step ahead of the nightmare that stalks him-a sentient, seething plague-entity that stalks its chosen prey: the last of the human race. To accept it is a living death. To defy it, a hell beyond imagining

"kick back and enjoy some the most violent and genuinely scary apocalyptic horror written by one of the finest dark fiction authors plying his trade today" HORRORWORLD

Lightning Source UK Ltd.
Milton Keynes UK
UKOW042350211112

202576UK00002B/4/P